C000261850

WICKED REJECTION

PREDATORS & PREY #1

SCARLETT SNOW

AUTHOR NOTE

Since I was a wee girl, I've dreamt of becoming an author. I had many people in my life tell me that my head was in the clouds and that I'd never become one. It was "just a hobby" or "not a real job". I am so grateful that you, my wonderful readers, helped me prove them wrong, and as a thank you for your support, I have 2 FREE BOOKS for you available to download here: https://books.bookfunnel.com/scarlettsnowfreebies

Happy reading!
~Scarlett

MAP OF ARITHYM

1

ZORIAH

A dark shadow appears behind me.

My stomach clenches when I take in their sombre reflection because I know I'm the cause of it. With his head slightly bowed and his eyebrows drawn together, Tristan has never looked more miserable than he does right at this very moment. He catches me looking at him and softens his features somewhat.

But it's too late.

I've already seen his reaction.

For the past twelve months, I've been promised to the Light Alpha, but Tristan has refused to acknowledge any of it until now. Now, he's escorting me to the mating ceremony himself, and I can only imagine how difficult it must be for him.

"You don't have to do this," I whisper. "There's still time."

He shakes his head and reaches for the only proof of my parents' existence: the gold necklace my dad gave my mom on their honeymoon. Everything else was left in the snow along with their bodies. .

Unclipping the chain and lightly draping it around my neck, Tristan says: "You are the alpha's mate. It's just that I'm..." He sighs and holds my gaze in the mirror. His soft tone contradicts the harsh lines etched on his forehead. "I just want you to be happy, Zo Bear."

My cheeks heat up, and I smile at him. He's called me this for as long as I can remember.

I caress the ruby, sun-shaped jewel resting in the valley of my throat and nod. "I will be happy. And who knows? Maybe Solas will still let us see each other. We are family at the end of the day."

Another shake of the head and strands of his dark hair fall into emerald eyes. "It won't matter. You know the rules. The alpha would never change them."

My reply dies on my lips because he's right. The rules of this pack clearly state that if an unmated male is found alone with the alpha's mate, they risk severe punishment. Even if I asked him, Solas would never break tradition. He thrives on them and obeys them religiously no matter how antiquated they are. And so utterly stupid. I mean, Tristan is like a brother to me. I'm hardly going to do anything with him.

"All right." His voice pulls me from my reverie. "You're ready."

He steps back, and I take a final look in the mirror. With my ivory skin, wavy silver hair, and the swan-white, silk dress spilling around my ankles, I look more ghostly than I'd like. I pinch my cheeks to get more color and then Tristan links my arm with his. With my best friend at my side, I make my way to the Mating Ceremony. My heart thrashes with each barefooted step toward the forest. The trees swaying in the cool breeze brush the twilight sky and stars flicker between the leaves. I take a deep inhale of the crisp air and breathe a sigh to calm my nerves.

This is finally happening.

And who knows, maybe I'll be the first one brave enough to alter pack custom. It's about time someone did. I just need to become the alpha's mate first and then my opinions will no longer be brushed aside. No one will laugh at me anymore.

Tristan squeezes my arm, a silent note of reassurance. It's as if he were reading my mind. I offer a smile in return and glance down at the candles lining the walkway into the forest. White rose petals dance around them, scattered intermittently. Everything is always white here as a symbol of purity, for being pure in a world of impurity is a custom my pack relishes the most.

I lift my gaze from the flowers to the sky again. The full moon sits proudly in the inky-black sky, but part of it is stained crimson. Blood on the moon is never a good omen. I swallow my unease and focus on the path ahead. A glance at Tristan does little to settle my nerves; his expression is clouded with worry. Of course, I'd be lying if I said I wasn't also worried. This is a big day for the two of us, and things will never be the same.

But I'm ready for this.

A fresh start.

My role as the alpha's mate.

After tonight's ceremony, our pack will be able to shift whenever they want to again. It's been so long since they've been able to do that. In fact, I don't even remember it and I've never been able to shift myself. But once I'm mated, everything will change: light wolves will be able to shift freely again as will I.

3

The path tapers the farther we venture into the forest. Lights appear distantly, seemingly floating among the trees, and low murmurs carry to my ears. In hearing them, my pulse settles enough for me to make out their voices.

They're as excited and nervous as I am deep inside.

No doubt they're desperate for the curse to be lifted so they can shift again.

Tristan pauses at the entrance of the clearing. He faces me then, and slivers of moonlight cut over his handsome features. There's a pained look on his gaze though that causes my heart to clench like a squeezed fist.

"Zoriah—"

"I want this. This is all I've ever wanted. Trust me."

Twigs snapping punctuate the silence, drawing our attention to the clearing. A robed figure stands waiting, his features masked in shadows.

"Come, sweet lamb. It is time."

The alpha's voice is deep and powerful, and goosebumps rise over my body. A shiver of desire runs through me. Although I have yet to feel the true mating bond between us, I've been assured it will come once we've bonded.

My heartrate picks up again, and in my excitement, I almost forget who holds my arm. I incline my head to the alpha and turn to my best friend. My voice catches in my throat a little.

"Thank you for everything."

Tristan reaches out. Pausing only briefly in response to the alpha clearing his throat, he ruffles my hair with a playful grin.

"Hey, you're going to ruin it," I say, adjusting my hair with a pretend scowl.

When the alpha extends his own hand, I withdraw from

Tristan and go to him.

Solas casts a dark glance in Tristan's direction, his silver eyes narrowing, then he looks back at me.

"Are you ready, Zoriah?"

My heart skips a beat with excitement and nerves.

"Yes, Alpha. I'm ready."

Side-glancing Tristan, he asks, "Ready for what, sweet lamb?"

I can't look at either of them when I reply. "To become your mate, Alpha."

His face softens and a lopsided grin upturns his lips. "Then let's go. The gods are waiting."

I bite my lip to keep from glancing back at Tristan and silently follow the alpha.

I'm doing this for us, Tristan. Hopefully, you'll one day realize that...

When we arrive at the clearing, the rest of the pack have gathered by the stone altar and are dressed in white ceremonial robes similar to the alpha's. They fall silent upon seeing our moonlit silhouettes. Candles decorate the stone altar to form the shape of a circle, a symbol of purity that's meant to protect those who bond within it. Every wolf who's come before us is said to gather and watch the claiming of a new alpha mate. I imagine my mother standing amongst them, and my father, whoever he was. The thought of their spirits watching should fill me with shame, but if anything, I feel only pride.

Out of all the other females in the pack, the Light Alpha chose *me*.

Solas leads the way to the front of the altar and, with our hands joined, turns to face our pack. The faces of those I've grown up with, men, women, and children stare back at me. A rapt silence grabs each of them and the only sound I can hear is that of my racing heartbeat.

"Lie upon the sacred altar."

I nod and lift my dress before climbing up. Solas takes my hand in his and gently eases me onto my back. He brushes my cheek, just a whisper of a caress, and then steps out of my peripheral. I keep my gaze fixed on the night sky draped over me, like a blanket of stars centered around a blood-stained moon. It's instantly calming, and I almost forget where I am.

The wax dripping down the side of my leg pulls me back, and I let out a surprised gasp. Solas walks around the altar and picks up one of the candles. He holds it up for the pack to see, which they cheer for, but not once does he look away from me.

"Let this spark the dawning of a new bond," he says, tilting the candle over my stomach, "and for its fire to never cease burning with the blessing of Nuala, Goddess of the Sun."

I bite my lip to keep from making a sound and simply watch him. He looks ethereal like this, standing over me with the moon casting him in a silvery glow. The smile he gives when he catches me looking makes my heart stutter in my chest.

He pulls back and exchanges the candle for a gold athame. The wolf-shaped handle glints in the light as he cuts into his palm. He smears his blood over my stomach, drawing an X, and I breathe a sigh of relief.

The alpha has officially marked me as his chosen mate.

He lets out a sigh, too, and once more caresses my cheek.

I lean into him and there's an intense yearning in his gaze that speaks of burning euphoria. The same emotion flares through me as I prepare to bond and become the alpha's mate. But then his eyes shift from silver into a deep crimson that I've never seen before.

"Now, my sweet little lamb," he says ever so calmly, "it is time for you to die."

2

ZORIAH

The last time I checked, dying wasn't part of the ritual. Or, in fact, any mating ritual known to shifters.

This I am absolutely certain of.

And yet, as Solas lifts the blood-stained athame over my heart, I'm consumed by a shock so paralyzing it leaves me frozen on the altar with a crippling inability to move or protect myself.

He pulls the athame down, but a loud warning howl stops his hand in the air.

It jolts me back into reality, and I push off the altar, rolling onto my side, seconds before a dark wolf lunges from the shadows; its gigantic body slams into Solas and drags him to the ground. A fist connects with the wolf's head, forcing it to the side, and for the briefest of moments, a familiar set of green eyes connect with my own. The star-shaped scar cutting through the right eye is exactly like Tristan's scar.

This wolf... is Tristan.

He snaps his head to the side and sinks his teeth into

the alpha's shoulder, cutting through the layers of skin like wet paper. Screams of horror and outrage break loose. No sooner does Tristan retract his fangs does he start snarling —at me. He throws Solas aside, nudges me to my feet, and motions for me to climb on. I don't hesitate. His enormous paws hit the ground running, and he charges into the trees. I hold on to his soft fur and move my body with his. The smell of blood engulfs my senses and then a metal object glinting in the light catches my attention.

Tristan is wounded somewhere.

I scan him quickly. My panic twists into gut-wrenching horror when I realize he's been stabbed by the very knife intended to take my own life. I grip his fur with a trembling hand stained in blood. With my steadier hand, I reach for the blade. Better to get this out quickly so he can heal. He growls when I touch it, the blue crescent moon on his forehead glowing brightly, but I pull it out anyway. He doesn't even yelp. His flesh immediately heals, but once more he growls, this time louder. It takes me a second to realize it's directed at the voices shouting in the near distance.

The voices of all those I trusted.

Voices belonging to the people I grew up with.

Now they're following the alpha's orders to find me and kill me before the sun rises. A smirk slides over my lips at the thought of them being unable to shift. They'll never be able to do it unless their alpha mates with his chosen mate and that boat just fucking sailed.

He stops on an outcrop that overlooks the clearing. I slip off his back and hide in the shadows, my senses instantly acclimating. Down below, Solas is being carried to a healer beside the altar while his betas bark out orders to find me. It will take them at least an hour to reach where Tristan has taken us in less than ten minutes, thanks to his wolf. It gives us enough time to figure out what the hell is going on and where to go next. Tristan shifts back into his male form, his naked body bathed in moonlight. He wipes the blood and sweat from his forehead and looks at me.

"What the fuck just happened?" I ask, staring him dead in the eye. "They just tried to fucking kill me!"

Those familiar lines of worry reappear, creasing his temple.

"No," he says, slowly shaking his head. "They tried to sacrifice you."

An abrupt chill slams through me, leaving an icy path in its wake that chills me to the bone. 'Sacrifice you' were definitely not the words I expected to hear.

"What..." My voice catches. "What do you mean?"

The words feel thick in my throat, but I manage to get them out.

Tristan clenches his jaw and grabs his hair. For a long while, neither of us speak. Only the sounds of our pack below fill the silence. When the noise starts to fade, telling us the alpha's sent a hunting party, he says something.

"Maya told me about the ceremony and why the alpha can only choose his mate on a Blood Moon. It's not to breed with. It's to sacrifice to the gods." His Adam's apple jerks. "Only once their blood bathes the earth can light wolves shift again."

"An eye for an eye," I say, my skin crawling as gut-wrenching reality dawns on me. "I knew our pack had to offer blood in exchange for shifting, but I never thought... I had no idea that... maybe something else... a different kind of blood."

My stomach heaves in gut-wrenching realization.

All this time, I've been kept here as nothing more than a

lamb raised for slaughter. And all this time, my best friend knew.

He knew and yet he lied to me.

"Why did you keep this from me?" I ask, my voice barely a whisper.

He looks up, his eyes gleaming in the moonlight. "Solas. He threatened to kill Maya and the pups if I told you. I didn't know what the fuck to do. I kept thinking I had time to come up with a plan, one that would get us all the fuck out of here, but then it was the day of the ceremony and I..." His voice breaks, forcing him to clear his throat and shake his head. "I just couldn't fucking stand there and watch him kill you."

Despite my shocked state, I crouch in front of him and look into his eyes. This is my best friend. Yes, he lied to me, and yes, it hurts to know he kept the truth to himself for so long. But his actions were done to protect those we both care deeply for. She's been like a mother to us since we were young. Her family became our family. A quiver catches my lip at the prospect of them being hurt.

"I would've done anything to protect them too. Do you really think Solas will stay true to his word? Maya's his sister."

Tristan shakes his head again. "Doesn't matter. What's done is done. We need to get the fuck out of here before he finds out."

I wrap my arms around him and pull him into an embrace. We sit like that for a moment, under the moonlit sky, while ceaseless thoughts rush through my head. Now isn't the time to think about Maya or how we can save her. If we don't save our own necks first, we won't be able to do anything. For now, we need to find somewhere safe to lie low before Solas or his precious mutts find us.

But where can we go? I pull back and tilt my head to study Tristan. Maybe he knows somewhere we can hide. We've never spoken about his past or why he's the only one in our pack who has dark hair. Every other wolf on this side of the realm are light-haired which is why, as children, bullies had often accused Tristan of being a spy for Shadowlands. The taunting became so bad Solas made a public announcement to put the rumors to rest and soon everyone moved on. The fact always remained, however, that Tristan isn't just part light wolf.

"Do you remember anything about where you came from?" I ask him, my voice low.

He falls quiet for a moment, his Adam's apple jerking a little. "I don't remember anything before your parents found me. All those memories, pleasant or unpleasant, are just... gone. It's like peering into fog when I think that far back." He glances away and falls quiet for a moment, but then, as if fishing out a memory he thought long had been forgotten, a weak smile pulls faintly at his lips. "But I remember the day we came here though. Your dad's boots left these giant holes in the snow, and I kept jumping through them. I can still hear your mum laughing when the snow nearly swallowed me up. That was just before..." He trails off, unable to voice what we both know happened next. "Look, I know how insane this is going to sound, but it might be our only shot at getting out here and..."

He turns and reaches up to squeeze the back of his neck, a nervous habit of his that instantly puts me on edge.

"What is it?" I ask, swallowing the sudden lump of trepidation in my throat.

Tristan turns back to me with a look of unyielding determination. "There's only one alpha who'd put their pack in danger if it meant killing Solas. Maybe if we go to them and—"

"Tristan... don't," I shout in a whisper. "If you're suggesting that we go to him for help... you're out of your fucking mind."

"Maybe I am," he agrees without even blinking. "Or maybe we're just shit out of options right now. There's no other option. Killian—"

"—murdered my parents!" Tears sting my eyes as my searing-hot rage rushes through my body. "That little day out in the snow, I was six months old, and you were just a kid yourself. My parents were unarmed but that monster Killian still slaughtered them like they were nothing then left the two of us to freeze to death like bags of trash. I would rather die out here than go to him for help."

Tristan lunges and swiftly takes my hands prisoner in his. "*You* might rather die but I took a vow long ago to always protect you, so for the love of all things starlight, try to think about all this rationally. You can't shift yet. We've got no food or resources. We'd never survive out here alone without the protection of a pack, and as far as I know, there's only one alpha out there who'd even consider helping us."

I clench my trembling hands and shake my head, refusing to accept the unacceptable. "We can't."

"Think rationally," he repeats in a softer tone, but there's still a firmness to it.

"There's nothing rational about this. Death is a better alternative to begging the man who destroyed our lives for help."

"Who says anything about begging?"

I blink up at him. "How can we not? Dark wolves would never welcome us into their territory unless we were grovelling at their feet. They're cruel, spineless, completely feral and..."

I slam my mouth shut, just managing to hold back what more I was going to say, which is that Tristan's behavior tonight proved everything I just said—even if his wolf was the thing that saved my life. Dark wolves are the most dangerous shifters of all. They hate everything about us. I'd have to beg for my life just to keep them from shredding me to ribbons the moment I set foot on their land. Then again, if they did kill me, the light wolves would be able to shift again. That just makes their enemy equally as powerful. However, if they kept me alive, they'd prevent light wolves from doing the very thing they crave most.

Shifting.

Tristan looks at me, the blood-stained moon reflecting in his eyes. "With you on their side, Zoriah, the dark wolves will be strong enough to hold territory outside of the Shadowlands. Defeating Solas and claiming his land is all Killian has ever wanted. He'd be crazy to turn us away."

As much as I want to disagree with him, Tristan is right.

I'm the queen to Killian's king; without me, he might never win. And Tristan and I might never leave this place alive.

"I'd be crazy not to go through with this, wouldn't I?"

Tristan's cheeks dimple into a smile. "Yeah. You would be, Zo Bear."

I groan and step around him. "Fine then. We'll make a deal with the Dark Alpha, but if he betrays us, Tristan, I will kill him this time."

Tristan nudges me playfully. "That's if I don't kill him first."

Grinning at him, I shove his shoulder, and together we make our way to the Drokadian Border.

3
KILLIAN

Nothing beats the scent of my enemy's blood spilled under the full moon.

I drag the twilight air into my lungs and savor the final screams for mercy that cut through the trees around me.

Fuck, it feels good to be out here again.

The adrenaline coursing through me is always at its strongest when there's a Blood Moon.

I'm at my strongest, and I pity any light wolf foolish enough to trespass into my land.

Those fuckers think they're superior to us and that we're nothing more than beasts. So, whenever I catch a light wolf invading my territory, I like to play the role of the beast well. It's what I'm good at.

"How many, Boone?"

My old friend yanks his knife out from the light wolf's throat and wipes the blood on his pants. "Looks like this was the last one, alpha."

He cocks his head, and the only distinguishable feature of his, buried under thick layers of blood, are his green eyes.

This fucker loves a good hunt more than anyone. It's the kill he enjoys the most though. While I prefer to breathe in the scent of my enemy's suffering, he quite literally prefers bathing in it. A bit too messy for my liking, but it's his bloodlust that got him the rank of second beta.

I turn my gaze skyward again. "Good. Now go get a fucking wash. You reek."

He chuckles and shrugs in my peripheral vision. "You know, I've been wondering what to refer to this signature look of mine. Freya calls it 'bathing in the blood of your enemy.' That's got a nice little ring to it, don't you think?"

"Well, it does suit a nut-job like you."

Boone clears his throat and raises a finger. "I prefer to be called an Extractor of Information. It makes me sound less..." He pulls out another knife from the corpse and shrugs. "...nut-job-like."

"Hm. So what information did you extract from that scumbag at your feet?"

Boone puts away his weapons with a sigh. "Nada. Little fuck just squealed like a bitch. They don't make these Light Wolves wolves like they used to."

I open my mouth, about to tease him for his lacklustre extraction skills, but footsteps echoing in the shadows nearby stop me.

"Alpha," Fenrik calls out, "we've got a problem."

"Now isn't that just fucking dandy?" I grumble. "What kind of problem?"

His tall figure steps out from the shadows of the trees. He nods respectfully at me. "A real pain in the ass one at the border."

Older than me by a few years, Fenrik rarely shows his feelings, so when I see the frown on his face I know something has gone wrong. Sure enough, his frown deepens as he walks over to me, telling me I'm in for a real nasty surprise.

I used to think my brother's lack of emotion was to hide his resentment when I became alpha. We all know he wanted to lead our pack, but bastards forfeit that right unless they're a full-blooded dark wolf.

Fenrik's blonde hair is proof enough of his mixed blood.

Probably why he never bothered to contest anything.

Besides, he's still my brother at the end of the day. The fact that he's the best beta our pack has ever known is enough to keep my doubts about his resentment at bay. For now.

I glance at Boone and jut my chin to the corpse, a signal for him to handle the rest of the cleanup, then I turn back to my brother. With a nod from me, he leads the way silently. We emerge through the trees some minutes later into a vast, open wasteland devoid of any signs of life. A thin mist coats the fire ravaged ground and the only source of light comes from the sky. This border is all that stands between the Shadowlands and the Dawnlands.

Fenrik gestures to where some of my men have gathered by the river. I sniff the air, picking up a strange, familiar scent, and my pulse accelerates. If this scent belongs to who I think it does, things are about to get real damn interesting.

With long, heavy strides, I march over while my men clear a path. Fenrik stands beside me as I peer down at the unconscious body sprawled by the riverbank. The magic in the water bathes her in a deep sapphire glow. Oh, it's her alright.

I'd recognize Zoriah Medley anywhere.

Fenrik turns to our healer. "Vin, any luck identifying her?"

Vincent shakes his head. "Not a clue. There's too much blood and facial swelling to say. She passed out just before you got here." He turns to me. "What do you want me to do, Alpha?"

I bend down and lift a strand of Zoriah's hair. The normally white strand is soaked in blood, and her pulse is faint in my ears. So close to death. So close to my revenge. But I'm not letting her die just yet. Zoriah's got a lot to answer for before that ever happens.

"She'll die if we leave her out here."

By all accounts, Fenrik is right; she won't survive dawn at this rate. But I don't like the note of concern in his voice. Tempting though it is to leave the female to die, I've waited a long time to pay her back for what she did to me.

I want to enjoy her suffering for as long as possible.

"Bring her back with us." I stand and wipe my hands on my pants, disgusted by the fact that I touched her. "I've got a nice little dungeon she can call her new home."

In response to the concerned whispers that break out between my men, I harden my features into a scowl and my disgust twists into searing anger.

"Now listen up, every fucking one of you!" I nudge Zoriah with the side of my boot. "This female is our motherfucking enemy. Anyone found treating her otherwise will be considered treasonous. Understood?"

My men are quick to nod their assent although Fenrik is last to do it.

Something tells me I'll need to keep an eye on him for a while.

I don't like the way he's looking at my prisoner.

Distaste lingers in the back of my throat when I enter the healing den three days later. To give any prisoner the luxury of a bedroom is laughable. To give it to Zoriah is just downright insulting. But Vincent insisted she needed access to the healing pools until her fever broke. Even then she barely made it. I knew she would though. This stubborn female wouldn't leave our realms knowing that I still drew breath. It's clear to me she's come back to finish what she started all those years ago. Unfortunately for her, I have no intention of dying just yet either.

I duck under the low entrance and step into the dimly lit room. Boone stands by the bed, twiddling a knife between his fingers, while Fenrik leans against the wall across the room, his face expressionless.

"Wait outside," I say, my eyes pinned on the she-wolf. "This could take some time."

They leave the room without a sound.

Although the female's lashes are lowered, her breathing alludes to the fact that she is in fact awake.

"Pretending to be asleep will not save you from me… Zoriah."

At the mention of her name, she shoots her lids open and turns her head to squint at me. I run my gaze over her slender body, her long, silver hair falling over the pillow, and her bright sapphire eyes looking up at me. She's still as beautiful as I remember, but how that pretty little face can be so deceiving and deadly. I know better this time.

"What's brought you back here, sweetheart?" I smirk

and slowly make my way beside the bed. "Decided to try and finish the job? I'll admit I've never met anyone else quite so determined to kill me. Or one who nearly succeeded... twice." My smirk melts into a scowl. "You better start talking."

Despite her silent glaring, her erratic pulse lets her trepidation slip. I take delight in the fact that she's frightened of me.

She'd be a fool not to be.

Her life is now in my hands. How the tables have turned.

I stand at the bottom of the bed and grind my jaw harder the longer her silence grows. My knuckles blanch from the pressure of clenching them as I hold her unwavering gaze. Always so fucking defiant, this one. Even as enemies, Zoriah has never learned her place in Drokadis, but that will soon change.

She's in *my* territory now, and she'll yield even if I have to force her to her knees.

"Speak. Now."

"It's not... to kill you," she whispers hoarsely. "I'm here because I need your help and I have nowhere else to go."

I release a breath that transforms into a scoff. "For a wolf to have nowhere to go means they've *really* fucked up. What did you do? You seemed awfully proud to be a light wolf the last time you tried to kill me. When was that again?" I rub my jaw and lower my head in false contemplation. "Ah, yes. The last eclipse, I do believe. Next to the Wyvern's Tavern. You shot me with a silver arrow." Absently, I reach for my neck and rub the scar she left, just above my jugular. "Nearly got me that time, babe. If I didn't despise you so much, I'd almost applaud your sheer fucking audacity for what you did that day. Not too bad an aim either."

A tinge of color rises to her cheeks. "You deserved everything and more for what you did to me."

I raise my hands in mock supplication. "Well, now, you've got me there. I have spent my entire life trying to wipe out your pack." I lower my voice into a growl. "And I will continue doing so until every member of my murdered pack has been avenged. To my reckoning, that's quite the sum now."

Her eyes narrow into slits, but she bites her tongue. The muscles in her jaw clench from the effort of holding back her retort. It pisses me off more than anything, and I cross my arms to keep from punching something.

"Let's cut to the chase. You need my help, and I need you dead. I've waited a long fucking time for it. So what could you possibly offer me to stop that from happening right now?"

She drags her lower lip between her teeth, and fuck if it doesn't make my cock hard. I scowl and make a mental note to kick myself in the nuts later. Desire is the *last* fucking thing I should feel for her. She's the scum of the earth.

My *enemy*.

And now my prisoner.

I'd sooner kill her than fuck her, so my dick better start listening.

"I offer you the very thing you've always wanted." Her soft voice pulls my focus back to her. "The head of my alpha. I can help you kill Solas. It's what you've always wanted, isn't it?"

I rub a hand over my jaw, scratching my stubble. Interesting that she would offer to betray her own alpha. For so long, I've wanted Solas' blood. Dreamt so vividly of it I could taste it on my tongue when I woke up. He talks about being pure and following the light when in actual fact he gets off on torturing innocent women and children.

I push the memory of my mother and sister's corpses to the back of my mind and harden my stare. While I do not need the female's help to defeat my nemesis, I'm at the very least curious to hear more.

"Why would you *offer* me your help, she-wolf?"

She glances up at the low ceiling, her expression shadowed by an unpleasant thought. "Because an enemy of my enemy is my friend. Is that not what the humans say?"

I chuckle and cock my head at her. "Apparently. Still doesn't answer my question though. What the fuck did Solas do to you?"

She doesn't even hesitate when she replies. "He betrayed me and took my best friend prisoner."

Now that grabs my attention.

I uncross my arms and wait for more, but the female hesitates. By the way the veins pulse in her temple, she's at war with herself on whether or not to answer me. Probably wondering if she should lie. She'll learn quickly that lying to me will only result in punishment—even for outsiders like her.

"Tell the truth, Medley, or I will personally drag you across the border on your ass. This is your only warning. Heed it."

She takes a sharp breath and holds it in for a moment. "Trust me, if I had someplace else to go, I wouldn't be here either. You're the last person I'd ever ask for help."

"And yet here you are. *Why*?"

A silence stretches between us, one in which I wait for

the female to break. She does eventually and with a reluctant sigh.

"Because I was never Solas' mate. I was just his blood offering to the gods." She lifts her lashes, glazed with unshed tears. "I bet you're just delighted to hear all this, aren't you?"

"Oh, come on now. Delighted isn't quite the word I would use..." I trail off, because in truth, I'm fucking ecstatic.

I have the light wolves' blood offering sitting in the palm of my hands. Rumor has it she's the last of her line. Without her, my enemy will never be able to shift again. They'll be weak and vulnerable, giving me the perfect opportunity to strike.

I could finally wipe them out.

My pulse skyrockets at the prospect. Fuck, this is good. Almost too good to be true. If what the female speaks of is the truth, she isn't a gift *to* the gods but rather a gift *from* them.

And it's been delivered straight to me.

"Say I did consider this, how would this even work?"

She wets her lips, her eyes intent on me. "You're the last person Solas would ever think I'd make a deal with." I scoff, but she continues with narrowed eyes. "My point is that you could use me as bait to lure him into a trap. Getting me back is the only way Solas would ever agree to meet you."

I run a hand over my smooth jaw and consider her words. Tempting though they are, there's something about her willingness to help me that doesn't quite add up. For all she knows, I could keep her in my own pack as a slave, a mere breeder forced to give me litter after litter. Her life could be made hell under me, and for good reason too, yet she's willing to do that just for me to kill the alpha who broke her little heart?

Mind you, this female has tried to kill me, on more than one occasion, for less. Perhaps her only motive is revenge. Still, I want to see how far she's willing to go to get it.

Would she risk me breaking her down to nothing?

I lean against the wall, folding my arms again. "What do you get out of this?"

Something tells me there's more to it than me killing her alpha.

The female's lashes flutter as she glances down. "My best friend back." The vein in her throat jerks from the effort of swallowing hard. "They helped me escape but were taken prisoner before we reached the border. They…" A quiver catches her lower lip, but she bites down to hold it back. "They were in bad shape. Saving them is what I get out of this. The fact that you kill my alpha is a bonus."

A grin tugs my lips. "So you want me to save your little friend, huh? How can you trust I'll do that once I've killed Solas?"

She glares up at me. "I don't trust you at all, dark wolf, but I don't have a choice… Do *you*?"

"Do I what?"

"Have a choice?" Before I provide an answer, she adds, "We both know you don't either, Killian. You would've killed Solas long ago if you did. That tells me you need my help."

"Need and want are two very different things."

"Not in our realm. We need what we want to survive, and we want what we need to be the ones on the top. It's a dog-eat-dog world out there."

"You're a smart wolf, I'll give you that," I say. As much as I despise her, she says things that have frequently crossed my mind. "But if you want me to save your friend, it'll cost you more."

"They banished me," she all but growls. "I don't have money. I've got nothing!"

"Temper, temper, little one. Did I say you would pay me in money?"

Her eyebrows lift before she pulls them downward into a grimace. She better stop biting her fucking lip or my cock might forget that I hate her.

"I have something else in mind. Something that is more priceless." I trail my gaze over her body with deliberate slowness, then I rest on her face. "You, Zoriah."

Blood rushes to her cheeks and stains them a delectable shade of pink. My message has clearly landed if this reaction is anything to go by. Good. She is indeed a smart wolf.

"What could you possibly want from me?" Her voice is just below a whisper, but there's an edge to it. Always an edge.

I quirk a brow. "If I told you, it would ruin the surprise."

She falls quiet, and I take a moment to glance out the window. The Temple of Ryviel, God of the Moon, gleams in the moonlight across the clearing. Thick, swaying trees shroud the building, and their swaying limbs cast eerie shadows across my land. While it may be considered a daunting sight to trespassers, this is home to the Blackwater Wolves.

Safety and refuge.

This temple is all we've got left of our natural habitat. The other buildings were burned down in a light wolf attack, leaving only the cabins and mess hall behind. It's because of Solas and wolves like him—wolves like Zoriah—that little of my pack's history remains.

I train my gaze back on Zoriah. "I've heard your terms,

female. Now it's time you heard mine. Let's go for a little walk, shall we?"

Before she can think to resist, I grab her by the arm and haul her from the bed. The door swings open with a wave of my hand, and the scent of burning leaves lingers in the air.

"Did you just use magic?"

"Perks of being the enemy your sun goddess so deeply despises," I growl, tugging her forward. "Keep up."

With that, I all but drag the female outside and across the clearing toward the temple. The building stretches over us, the crescent moon spires reflecting the light. Members of my pack move aside to watch me thrust open the crimson doors and drag the female over the threshold.

"You want my help? You want me to save your friend and kill your alpha?" I do not wait for a reply and simply continue dragging her to the altar at the end of the aisle. "Then you better start getting used to living here, female, because you're going to be here a long time."

She yanks her hand from my grasp, though in truth, I was about to let go. When I pivot to face her, she moves into a combative stance, her fists clenched to protect herself. Or fight me. A smirk stretches over my lips at the thought of her daring to challenge me, here of all places. I could kill her with my bare hands if I wanted to, snap her neck like a chicken.

But killing her would be showing her mercy. No. I have something else in mind, something that will make her regret the day she ever tried to kill me.

"I'm not living here," she hisses, her eyes wide and unblinking.

"Ah, but if we make this deal, you won't be leaving. You'll be stuck here for the rest of your life as... my..." I pause deliberately, taking great delight in the way her heart thrashes like a caged bird. "...mate. Is that something you could truly do? Give yourself freely and willingly to the very wolf you've spent your whole life despising?"

She doesn't even blink. "I wouldn't be here if I wasn't willing to sell my soul to the devil himself."

The edge of my mouth twitches. "I don't want to buy your soul. I want to bind."

"But... why? Why choose me as your mate?" she whispers.

I close the distance between us. "Because as you so brilliantly put it, an enemy of my enemy is my friend. Now she's going to be my mate and the mother of my pups."

That gets the reaction I wanted—deep, burning hatred that she doesn't bother suppressing or covering up this time.

"And if I don't want to be your mate?"

I shrug, although a tinge of anger surges through me. "Then you'll remain here as my prisoner. Either way, you're not going anywhere, sweetheart." Glancing briefly over at the altar, I add, "You have until the next full moon to make your choice. If you've chosen right, when that night comes, I'm going to claim you right here on that altar. You'll be mine and only mine. Forever."

She raises her head and looks me dead in the eye. Brave for a female. And reckless. "Do whatever you want. Claim me. Imprison me. Just kill my alpha once and for all."

I smirk and tilt her jaw, forcing her to look at me.

"I'm your alpha now, little mate, and I'm going to make you wish you never stepped into my land."

4
ZORIAH

His lips crush against mine, spearing my mouth with ruthless determination. In my shock, I all but surrender to him, letting my body go limp. I keep my gaze locked on his closed lids, my eyes wide and unblinking, while he threads a hand around my throat and pulls me closer. My body presses into his chest as the air is sucked out from my lungs by this viper before me.

The creaking of doors opening returns me to reality, and I push with all my might away from him. His pupils are blown, dilated with an unhinged, animalistic lust that both repulses and excites me.

"Not bad." A grin stretches over his lips as I glare at him, wiping my mouth with the back of my hand. "Though I do look forward to kissing your other lips too."

Over my dead. Fucking. Body.

It's already unbearable to think that my worst enemy wants to mate with me. Words fail to reach my mouth. It's as if he really has siphoned the air out from my entire body. Footfalls thudding toward us draw the alpha's attention away. He nods once, then turns back to me.

"Until then, you will be treated like every other outsider." He gestures to the male behind me. "Take her to the dungeons."

Fenrik, the beta wolf who had been there when I woke up in the sick room, stops beside me. His face is wiped clean of emotion. He takes me by the arm and motions me forward.

I glare over my shoulder at Killian. "Do you treat all your allies like prisoners?"

His lips twist into a cruel smile. "Only the ones who try to kill me."

Before I can so much as utter a reply, I'm taken from the chapel and dragged back to my prison. Well, what did I really expect would happen? Killian may have agreed to help me defeat a common enemy but that doesn't make him my friend. Hell, I'd never want him to be. I would sooner kill him if given the chance. Once he helps me rescue Tristan, that is, then it's back to me trying to eradicate him.

Fenrik pushes the doors open and once more I'm thrust into the eyes of those who hate me. Members of the pack stop in their tracks to stare at me as if I'm an exotic creature trapped in an exhibit for their perusal. But they're looking at me, not with mild curiosity, but sheer and utter disdain. Not that I can really blame them.

We're enemies at the end of the day, and their condition of living is damn near uninhabitable compared to the Dawnlands. No wonder those in the Shadowlands have always resented us. While Solas and his followers have been living like kings, the dark wolves have barely managed to scrape by. I actually feel sorry for them in a way and that's not something I ever expected to feel for my enemy.

Why did their God desert them like this, anyway?

I blink up at the starlit sky and squint my gaze against

the moonlight. Ryviel represents all the things I've been raised to suppress. Carnage. Chaos. Carelessness. I've watched dark wolves hunt from afar and there has always been a part of me that felt envious. They were so free compared to us. So in touch with their wolf side that it was almost painful to watch them chase each other through the woods. Now they're looking at me like I'm the prey.

I suppose, in a way, I am to them.

Even in spite of the nervous twisting of my stomach, I lift my gaze high and look ahead as I follow the beta. He leads me past the rows of dwellings built into the trees. The wooden roofs are shrouded in thick canopies of luscious green leaves twined with straw. At the end of the path stands a building of incredible size. It must have been some kind of grand fortress long ago. Now it's derelict and neglected in some areas.

The entryway towers over me as I'm none too gently guided through it. The stone passageway leads down to what appears to be a cellar of some kind. It's not until I'm thrust over the threshold and my eyes adjust to the low lighting that I realize it's a dungeon.

A poorly maintained one at that.

Fenrik retrieves a set of keys from his coat pocket and shoves a gold one into the lock.

With a twist that makes me flinch, the gate opens and the beta stares at me to go in.

"This is... where I'll be staying?" I ask, unable to hide the horror in my voice.

His face shows nothing. "Aye. This is where you'll be staying."

He stands back and watches me creep into the dungeon. It's the first time he's spoken, and his deep, husky voice has a note of danger that seems to be mirrored on his face. A sudden chill sweeps over me, and I rub my arms. My breath comes out in puffs of smoke.

"It's h-homey," I say through chattering teeth. "C-could do with some feminine t-touches though. Maybe a nice rug to cover up some of the—the blood. Or is that damp? I'm just gonna tell myself it is."

Something flashes in his blue eyes—humor, maybe?—but it vanishes as quickly as it appears. He slams the gate shut, and I wince at the vibrations that echo around me. As the beta turns and makes his way back up the stairs, I slide down to the floor, my arms pressed close to my chest. Tears threaten my eyes, but I shake my head, refusing to let a single droplet fall. Tristan would've done this for me. If spending the rest of my life in this dungeon guarantees his freedom, I'll do it.

I'll do anything to save him—even mate with Killian.

The door opens again and Fenrik reappears, carrying what looks to be a collar of some kind. He doesn't even look at me when he opens the gate and steps inside, ordering me to lift my head.

"You can't be serious? He's collaring me?"

The male bends down to my eye level. "The alpha doesn't want you shifting and trying to run away. Now look up."

Despite the rapid churning of my stomach, I tilt my head toward the ceiling. Droplets of something drip down and splash my cheek. I swallow hard as the collar is latched around my neck, the iron thick and heavy. Enough to remind me of my place here. Not that being caged wasn't a clear enough reminder.

The thing is, the collar is pointless with me. I wasn't alive during the last solar cycle, so the Goddess of the Sun didn't bless me with the ability to shift. I've never seen what my shifter form looks like. Is she grey, like most of the light wolves? Or is she white like my mother had supposedly been?

I don't confess to the wolf that I'm unable to shift. The fact that they want to use precautions with me swings in my favor. It means the alpha hasn't forgotten what I'm capable of doing. Even if, at this moment, all I care about is rescuing my best friend.

I lift my legs and wrap my arms around them, watching as the beta straightens. His boots linger in my vision as he pauses for a moment, apparently watching me too, then he locks the gate and leaves.

So this is my new home...

As a rat scuttles in the far corner of my cell, I pray to the gods to let Tristan still be alive.

5
ZORIAH

S*ome days later*

"Wake up, female. You've got a big day ahead of you."

Fenrik's deep, husky voice pulls me from the only place I'm safe to be myself again. To be free. For the past week, my position as Killian's prisoner has been made abundantly clear. Meals consist mostly of dried meat, bland clumpy oatmeal, and water. Baths are by far the most degrading thing of all, if you can even call what I get a bath. I mean, being hosed down like an animal is the most dehumanizing experience I've ever been forced to endure. And that's saying something.

I squint up at the blinding sunlight pouring through the solitary window carved into the ceiling. Pain instantly stabs my eyes, and I shut them again with a groan. Several days confined to darkness with only rats for company has made me despise the sun now.

How ironic for a light wolf.

"Time to get up," Fenrik says, nudging the gate with the tip of his steel-capped boot. "The alpha's got something planned for you.'

"Is it matching shackles to go with my collar?" I scoff and push up into a sitting position, my gaze still averted from the sun. "Because I'd rather go without."

I dig my fingers into the blanket underneath me. Doing so has become an almost self-soothing coping mechanism I picked up a few days ago. The blanket appeared then, draped over me in the morning, and it's the only thing that offers a semblance of warmth.

Fenrik shakes his head. "You'll be glad to know it's not a punishment but a reward."

"Why would Killian reward his prisoner?" I ask, lifting my gaze.

His lack of response tells me he has no intention of elaborating. Not that I'm overly surprised anymore. I've become used to the beta's nearly impenetrable silence. I actually prefer it over the girl who dumps my meals outside the gate three times a day. Her visits are almost always accompanied with muttered insults which usually end up with Fenrik barking at her to leave.

Sighing, I push off my pathetic excuse for a bed and grab the blanket. I drape the material over my shoulders to keep warm and cross the length of the dungeon. My bare feet slap against the damp ground. It must have rained during the night. That explained why I'm still shivering.

I rub the lingering chill from my arms and wait by the gate. Once Fenrik has unlocked it, he leads the way down the hallway to where a grumpy-looking guard stands by the exit. He opens the door and nods respectfully at Fenrik, who curtly returns it and steps outside.

Shielding my eyes against the blinding light, I wait for my vision to acclimate before joining him. The fresh air hits me first and then the smell of meat grilling nearby. I take in deep lungfuls and scan the horizon. It's not morning at all. It's already dusk and the sun has nearly dipped behind the horizon.

"How long was I out for?" I ask the beta.

He doesn't look back when he answers. "Long enough to miss your meals."

"Oh, darn it," I mutter under my breath.

However, a quick glance at the wolves glaring around me instantly seals my mouth. Based on their living conditions, food of any kind is hardly to be scorned at.

"Dawnland scum," a male spits as I walk by.

Despite the scornful eyes following my every step, I keep my gaze pinned forward and follow the beta to whatever fresh hell awaits me next. He leads me into a semi-derelict building and the warmth that hits me when I enter is immediate.

Fenrik marches me down a tiled hallway and stops outside a door with condensation covering the glass. He opens it and a cloud of fragrant smoke envelopes me. It wraps around my body like a net and pulls me in like the call of a siren. When my gaze lands on the pool integrated into the floor, I know I'd surrender myself willingly to the siren's death song if only for a dip in the rose-tinted water.

"Towels are over there," the beta says, drawing my attention away from the beauty of the pool and back over to his ever-expressionless face. "You have thirty minutes. Suggest you make good use of it."

I practically gawk at him. "You mean this is for me?" The scents from the oil infuse my senses. "Why?"

35

"The alpha wants you cleaned up for when he sees you."

A cold dread sticks in my throat even when I try to swallow it. There's only one thing that could possibly mean, but I don't really want to think about it right now. Not when I'm being tempted with the luxury of a proper bath. Something I always took for granted back home.

I inhale sharply and step toward the pool. With the blanket still wrapped around my body, I glance over my shoulder at the beta.

"Are you just going to stand there and watch me bathe?"

His only answer is a smirk.

"Pervert," I mumble, turning back to the water.

If I've only got thirty minutes to enjoy a bath, I'm not going to waste it demanding some privacy.

I drop the blanket and fold it neatly beside the pool, out of reach so it doesn't get wet, then I slip off my dirty, blood-stained dress. I bundle the material into a ball and launch it across the room. It flutters into a heap beside one of the closed off pools, and a satisfied smile creeps onto my lips. It's the first I've been without that disgusting rag since I put it on for the ceremony. Hopefully, when this is all over, I can burn it along with Solas' corpse.

Ignoring the beta watching from behind, I climb into the pool and slowly lower myself down. My skin tingles, and I unconsciously let out a moan. There must be some kind of healing properties in the salts. My bones are no longer sore, and I can move again without experiencing any tenderness or pain.

Gods, this feels so good.

I wade through the pool to the other side and dip under, soaking my entire body underneath the surface.

I reach the other side and then fall onto my back. The water cradles me as I float and close my eyes, simply enjoying the privilege of no longer being uncomfortable. Obviously, this bath is for a specific reason. If Killian just wanted me to be clean, he'd have had someone hose me down like an animal. But these oils, the luxury shampoo, fluffy towels hanging on the railing, even the healing salts... they each serve a purpose in which I have no doubt is for the alpha's selfish gain instead of mine.

Honestly? I can't even bring myself to care right now.

All I want is to close my eyes and forget, so I do. I swim around, doing various laps, and then I grab the shampoo. Pouring a generous amount into my palm, I lather my hair. Finally I can wash the blood from the ceremony away. I don't even know if it's my blood, Tristan's, or Solas. A sick part of me hopes for the latter.

"Time to go."

I stand in the water and look over my shoulder again. Fenrik is by the pool, facing me, of course, with his arms crossed over his chest. Not a hint of emotion on his boldly unashamed face. The guy never seems to smile or give anything away. A towel hangs from his left hand which he extends to me.

I step out of the pool and wrap myself in it then pick up my blanket. Fenrik's eyes slide from the object to my face and there's something undetectable in his gaze. Almost... sympathetic.

"Through here," he grumbles, taking off in the opposite direction.

My feet slap against the tiled floor as I follow him. He leads the way into another room with wardrobes, dressers, and mirrors spaciously positioned. An unlit fireplace lingers in the near corner, and above the mantle hangs a portrait of a beautiful woman with twilight hair and bright green eyes. The tapestry is strangely the only piece of furniture with any dust on it. Even the perfume bottles appear to be recently cleaned.

"What is this place?" I ask, clutching the blanket and towel to my chest.

He closes the door behind me. "My mother's room."

"Is she the woman in the portrait?"

A single, curt nod that tells me to cease talking about her. Either something bad happened to her or she's no longer part of the pack. It's clear in the way Fenrik's expression darkens at the mention of her.

"Why are you doing this?" I ask quietly, barely audible even to my ears. I mean, I doubt his alpha will appreciate him being nice to his little prisoner, but I bite my lip to refrain from speaking.

I don't want to make Fenrik regret helping me.

The beta shrugs dismissively. "Alpha's orders were to get you ready. He didn't specify how or where." He flicks his chin toward the wardrobe and dressers. "Thought it's high time you got out of those stinking rags. Now hurry up."

An unexpected smile dances over my lips. I wonder if he left the blanket as I tiptoe over to the wardrobe and open the door. Beautiful dresses hang on the railing. The styles are simple and timeless, and shoes rest on a shelf above them.

I pull out a silk dress and check the label. It's exactly my size. The shoes are a little too big, but I'm grateful to wear anything at this point, so I slip them on once I slide the dress over my body. The emerald material clings to me like a second skin and the plunging necklace is crisscrossed with intricate ribbons. It's beautiful. I smooth a hand down the front of the dress, oddly reminded of when I'd prepared for the ceremony. Tristan had been standing behind me as Fenrik is right now.

"How do I look?"

The words slip from me before I can catch them and déjà vu washes over me.

In the mirror, Fenrik roves his gaze slowly over my body. "Ready for the alpha to see you. Follow." He moves to grab the blanket off the dressing table.

I snatch it up, saying quickly, "I'd like to take it with me... please."

He arches a brow but hands me the blanket all the same. I feel like a child holding her little 'blankie.' So silly. But there's just something soothing about it that the thought of not having it when I see Killian is like being stripped of the last thread of my identity.

Fenrik nods once and leads the way outside again. Some minutes later, I'm standing outside a dark wooden door in a hallway at the back of the temple. Fenrik knocks once, opens the door, and then shoves me over the threshold. He slams the door behind me with the finality of a lid sealing me within a coffin, only I'm still breathing.

For the most part.

Killian's scent fills my lungs as I take a deep, shaky breath and search the dimly lit room. As if drawn to him by a magnetic force, my gaze lands on the alpha seated at a large dining table. The surface has been set for two, with candles, silverware, and bottles of wine included. I don't acknowledge the huge four-poster bed placed on a platform under a stained-glass window. I keep my eyes pinned on Killian.

The moment he raises his head, I know something is wrong.

His smirk melts from his face and in its place a look that contorts his features into a sinister grimace.

"The fuck?" His chair scratches the floor as he pushes back and shoots up. "What the fuck are you wearing?" Dark eyes narrow on my dress. "Get it off!"

I lift my chin to look him in the eye. "Not even going to offer me a drink first, Alpha?"

His scowl deepens, and in a series of blurred movements, he shifts to my side.

I instinctively tense and prepare to defend myself. The look of murder burning on the alpha's face can hardly be a good sign. When he's within arm's reach of me, I clench my hands into fists, but he merely inspects my dress. He slides his gaze over me as though disgusted by what he's seeing.

"Where did you get this?" he growls, pulling at the ribbon tied at the valley of my throat.

I snatch the lace from him and step back. "Your flirtation skills are abhorrent, Alpha Killian. Is this how you usually compliment women?"

The pulse in his temple thrashes with ire. "You have no fucking right to wear this. Take it off!"

"What the— What are you do—!"

My words are cut off by his hands ruthlessly seizing my body. In one powerful motion, he rips the dress clean off, and his breathing has increased, heavy and fast. His incinerating eyes latch onto me.

"No. Right," he hisses through clenched teeth, his usually obsidian eyes a deep, burning crimson.

"No right to what? Wear clothes?" I choke out, mustering what words I can despite my frustratingly shocked reaction. "Even prisoners have the right to cover themselves up."

Flecks of crimson flash in his obsidian eyes. "My prisoners have no rights unless I grant them." He holds up the dress. "And this, I did not grant, but the one who did will be dealt with accordingly"

I bite my lower lip, not wanting to throw Fenrik into the ring of fire. He is the only one who's shown me any kindness. I hardly want to pay him back by betraying him. Killian returns to the table and sets the dress on a vacant chair. I burn a hole into the back of his skull, wishing more than ever that looks could indeed kill, and watch him settle down in his chair. He rests his arms along the edges like a king seated before his court. To think that if I were his queen, I would have him guillotined and his head mounted on a wall.

"You have an unusual way with prisoners," I say, cutting my gaze to him.

A smirk threatens his lips. "How so?"

I gesture to the dining table. "This, for starters. Captors do not usually dine with their prisoners."

He slams a fist suddenly on the table, jolting me. "And prisoners do not usually dress up in the captor's dead mother's clothes! You have a lot of fucking nerve to parade around in her dress after what Solas did to her."

His bellow echoes around the room, but the words give me pause. So this is why he freaked out about me wearing the dress. It belonged to his mother, and Solas was the one who killed her. While Killian's reaction makes sense to me now, stripping me naked the way he did is still a dick move. He could've just told me to change back into my own clothes, filthy though they were, and I'd have done it.

I grab my blanket off the floor and wrap it around my body. Tucking the edge between my breasts, I walk over to the table with slow, graceful strides. Killian doesn't even look up when I take the seat at the other end of the table.

He just continues staring into his whiskey before throwing it down in one large gulp. In front of me, a delicious smell creeps out from under a silver dish, and my mouth waters. It's with effort that I swallow down my hunger and force myself to look at the alpha. He's already watching me through the bare slit of his narrowed eyes. The dark pools shadowed by his thick lashes cut through me like a knife scoring meat, causing my heart to lunge involuntarily against my ribs.

I clear my throat and lift the dish, revealing a delicious-looking meal of veg and meat.

"I always wondered why you hated Solas so much," I say quietly, trying to break the tension percolating between us. "Now it makes sense. He killed your mother, didn't he?"

Killian scoffs and pours another whiskey. "I didn't bring you here to piss me off, sweetheart, but you're going the right way about it."

I draw my features into a scowl. "Then why did you bring me here, Killian?"

He shrugs. "Figured now you've seen what it's like to be my prisoner, you'd want a taste of what it's like to be my mate."

A bitter scoff escapes me as I reach for the silverware at either side of the dish. "Then I must inform you, Alpha, that so far your mating skills have been rather lacking." I take a small bite of the meat and swallow quickly. "Ripping my clothes, without even offering me a drink, was hardly chivalrous of you."

He raises his glass and winks at me over the crystal rim. "There is nothing chivalrous about me, sweetheart. The sooner you accept that, the better your life here will be."

"Oh, believe me, I already know all this. Your hosting has also been somewhat lacking." My stomach grumbles again, causing the alpha's brow to raise. "What happened to your mom?"

I voice the question more to distract myself from the food taunting me. The saliva pooling in my mouth is nearly seeping through my lips. *Damn it.* I don't think I've eaten a single thing all day, and it shows thanks to the dying sounds coming from my stomach.

Killian huffs and lifts his own dish, revealing a huge slab of rare meat. Nothing else. "You wouldn't have the stomach to eat if I told you," he says. "So I suggest you sit and wolf that down first, then we'll talk."

In spite of my curiosity, the hunger gnawing at my insides is becoming unbearable.

We begin the meal in silence. He keeps his focus on me, but I pretend not to notice while I tuck into the steak and roasted vegetables. My mouth waters with every bite, and for a while I completely forget where I am or who's company I'm in. All I can think, taste, see, and smell is the food in front of me. I've often taken it for granted. Never again will I do that.

Pouring a glass of red wine beside me, Killian draws my attention back to him. I didn't even hear him move. He's still looking at me as he sets the glass down. His eyes rake me slowly as though divesting me of every layer of skin. With a smirk, he saunters back to his side of the table and calmly resumes his place. Blood pounds through my ears. Why is it that everything about Killian, even just his breathing or the way he looks at me, makes me want to beat the living daylights out of him?

That's not what angers me the most though.

It's the way my pulse sometimes spikes whenever I meet his gaze.

I should be sickened by the way he looks at me, as if I'm

just a rare cut of meat ready for him to devour, but my heart continues to betray me. What the fuck? Maybe it's because the burning-hot rage I've harbored for him my entire life has finally reached its bubbling point. That's the only explanation as to why my heart refuses to function as normal.

"You know something?" he says, wiping his mouth with a napkin.

"I know many things," I spit back.

He smirks and cuts his eyes to my neck. "The collar. It suits you."

I blow air out from my nose in a derisive laugh. "Yeah, and it's the perfect size, too, almost like it was custom made for me."

He scoffs but doesn't confirm whether or not that's true. Hell, I wouldn't be surprised if he did have a collar created for me after I tried killing him the first time. I don't imagine being shoved into a magical portal where bunny rabbits are twenty-feet-tall and hold an intense, burning rage for wolves was any fun for him. I suppose being thrown into an alternate universe where you're the prey for once would bring out vengeful aspirations in anyone, even a saint, which Killian is certainly not.

He's the devil in disguise with a disposition that for centuries has been engineered to embrace the darkness. He doesn't even try to hide who or what he is.

He revels in it.

Just looking at his smug face makes me want to gut his eyes out with my knife.

Don't humans say that the third time's a charm? Maybe I should give it another—

"Penny for your thoughts, she-wolf?"

I twirl the knife between my fingers while lifting my lashes. "You wouldn't be able to eat if I told you, Alpha."

A slightly terrifying smile spreads over his wine-stained lips. "Try me." When I don't speak, he continues calmly: "Very well then. I'm going to hazard a guess you were thinking about taking your knife and running it through my throat. Is that not so?"

I shake my head. "I'm a lot more creative than that."

He rubs his throat absently. "Mm. I remember."

As if the memory has dragged him into the past, a dark look twists his features into a scowl, and a crease forms between his brows.

"I wasn't just thinking about killing you," I admit, taking a sip of my drink.

He grunts at that, though his dark expression remains. "Then what else were you pondering in that head of yours, little one?"

"How you escaped the bunny hell portal."

Killian blinks at me, then he grins and rubs his jaw. "I'll give you your dues, it wasn't easy. In fact..." He lifts his right hand and winks at me with clear, salacious intent. "...it damn near cost me my good hand. Now *that* I will never forgive you."

Despite my best efforts, laughter builds in my chest and a little burst of it escapes through my lips, causing me to almost choke on my water. I set the glass down and wipe my mouth with the back of my hand.

Across the table, the alpha studies me through heavy-lidded eyes. "You know what, I think it's time for dessert." He stands and circles the table, making his way toward me.

He moves with the slow, deliberate grace of a wolf stalking its prey. My pulse spikes, and I grasp the knife, preparing to attack him in self-defense. However, when he reaches my side, he only lifts a strand of my slightly damp hair and drapes it over my shoulder.

"Stop touching me," I hiss in a whisper.

Killian slides his fingers under my chin and forces me to look at him. "If I wanted to fuck you, Zoriah, you best believe that I'd have done it by now and you would've loved every goddamn second of it. As it stands, the thought of putting my cock in a light wolf's cunt doesn't quite get me off right now, so you'll just have to be a good little girl and be patient for my cock."

I scoff at him, scarcely able to comprehend the insanity of his words. He's lost his freaking mind.

"Who says I even *want* you?" I snarl at him.

His lips twist into a cruel smirk. "This right here." He thrusts a hand between my legs and roughly grabs my sex. "I could smell your cunt getting wet for me across the room." He leans in and inhales my neck, my hair, while squeezing and rubbing me with his rough hands. "Fuck, you smell amazing. It's like violets trapped in the snow, desperately clawing for a way out to reach the sunlight again. To be free." His lips brush the shell of my ear. "I bet that's what you want more than anything, isn't it? Your freedom back?"

My chest rises unevenly and the air thickens in my lungs. Still, I part my lips and try to push out the words. "I..."

But they all fail me.

My entire body fails me.

Under the cruel duress of his slow exploration, my body responds to him as though by my own admission. As though I want him to be doing this. The most terrifying factor of all is that at this very moment, I do want him to touch me.

I don't want him to stop.

"I bet you'd give anything to be free again," he whispers, circling my clit with the pad of his thumb. "From me. Is that so, little mate?"

I suck in a breath and surrender myself, *not* to Killian but to the pleasure he's bringing me. Already the rush of tingling heat gathering within my body intensifies between my legs. But then Killian stops and his withdrawal plummets my orgasm.

"Answer me. Is... that... so?" He repeats each word slowly, and when I give a single nod if only to feel that sensation again, he continues touching me. I squeeze my legs, but he parts them and places a hand on my thigh. "Then submit. Submit to me as your mate, and I'll give you everything you've ever wanted. Solas. Revenge. A pack. Even your little lover boy."

"But Tristan isn't— He's not my lo..."

My retort all but dies unuttered as the pleasure shooting through me makes it impossible to string a coherent sentence together. There's only stars, millions of them, dancing over my line of sight, and the wonderful crescendo that's building at my core.

"I'll agree he's never fucked you," Killian says, "because this"—he slides a finger inside me, then runs another over my opening—"is a virgin cunt. One I have every intention of filling when the full moon rises. You're already mine, Zoriah." His warm breath, tinted with whisky, fans my heavily flushed cheeks. "You'd be happier here if you just accepted that, little mate, so do it. Accept and yield to me. You know you want to."

"N-no..."

The alpha pauses, both hands frozen on my body. "What was that?"

"I said no," I snap, looking up at him. "You gave me a choice and a date in which to decide my fate. Until then, I belong to neither you nor anyone else out there. My freedom is my own, to do with as I please, and right now, it would please me very much if you just backed the fuck off and let me breathe. Is that so much to ask?"

An unusual look of awe flits over his face. He pulls back and regards me through mildly amused eyes. Technically, my whole freedom spiel isn't entirely true since I am after all being treated as a prisoner under Killian's command. Still, I hold my ground regardless of how unstable my footing might be at this moment. I need him to realize how serious I am and that there's nothing I won't do to save Tristan. He's more than my best friend.

He's the shadow that's followed my whole life, always looking out for my safety.

Now it's my turn to repay the favor, even if it means paying for it with my own life. Although, at this precise moment, Killian doesn't look like he wants to kill me.

He looks as if he would much rather eat me... possibly *out*, if his dark gaze drinking me in and the subtle jerking of his Adam's apple are indicators to go by. For some reason, it makes my insides flutter, and I rub my thighs together to the image of his mouth on my clit, his tongue sliding over my lips, gently kissing, sucking, nibbling, teasing...

A sudden chill cuts through me and jolts me back to reality. However, with this return also comes deep, devastating awareness to the fact that not only did I fantasize about Killian, my captor and my enemy, but I wasn't sickened by it like I once would have been. That alone is enough to remind me of the reason why I'm here.

Tristan.

Ignoring the slight tremor in my throat, I hold Killian's gaze, "I know what it is you want from me."

He smirks slowly and seductively. "I want many things from you, female. You'll need to be more specific."

I lower my gaze and focus on my hands clasped on my lap. "You want me to surrender and give myself willingly to you. You don't want a prisoner. You want a mate, and for whatever reason, you want that to be me." I lift my lashes and look him dead in the eye. "But we both know I will never choose to be your mate if you can't even provide me with proof of Tristan's safety."

He leans in with a slow, seductive smile stretching over his lips. "The fact that you'd dare voice demands of any kind, let alone in your position, continue to prove how in over your head you are in my pack. Naivety in my pack is one thing. To make demands of the very alpha who holds the key to your freedom is another entirely."

He lifts the fingers he had moments before shoved inside me and brings them to his lips.

"Throw in the fact that you stopped him from enjoying his favorite meal?" He pauses long enough that I'm forced to inhale my own scent. "Now that's just looking for trouble, baby girl."

Without even blinking, he licks his fingers as though I were a rare delicacy intended for him alone. Blood assaults my cheeks under his visual duress, and I curse my inability to suppress my own embarrassment. That's just the reaction he wanted.

Killian, on the other hand, continues smirking at me. Not once does he look away from me, not even when he steps back to lean against the side of the table. He cocks his head in my direction and looks down his nose at me. The vein pulsing in his throat and the side of his temple contradicts his seemingly calm exterior, and it makes me smile. Clearly, he's annoyed with me and that brings a little comfort.

He catches me smiling and pinches his eyes. "Look, even if I did consider your demands, they could not be easily met in such a short time," he says, then he wets his lips in a deliberately slow motion and moans deep in his throat, savoring my taste. He grins when I flush again. *Damn him!* However, this time, I refuse to look away. "As you well know, the heart of the Dawnlands is not easily penetrated. I need time to plan an attack, one that now involves a rescue operation. This all takes time, sweetheart, and patience."

My heart plummets to the pit of my stomach. "I have patience. Tristan doesn't have time. Don't you get it? Every second is life or death for him."

Killian's features do not move. "He will be rescued soon enough."

I dig my nails into my palm, nearly drawing blood in a fruitless effort to mask my rage. However, the blood boiling in my veins pounds with a violent and furious intent that drowns out my other senses. If that's all I can hear, Killian can hear it too. I might end up regretting my next words, but I've had enough.

"A true alpha always honors their word," I say, the words pouring out my lips before I can plug them. "The fact that you do not stay true to yours means that you're not an alpha. You're a liar and a coward."

A powerful gust of air sweeps over me, and within the blink of an eye, Killian has seized my chin between his fingers. He roughly forces me to look up and meet his incinerating gaze. My stomach clenches in response to the fury burning in his black, soulless eyes.

"I will stay true to my word when I am good and ready," he growls, his deceptively calm voice steeped in dangerous intent. He adds just the slightest bit of pressure to his grip. "And not when you say so."

I swallow back my unease and allow the bluff to flow from my lips. "Then you're the one who needs to wait. Lock me up in your cage, throw away the damn key for all I care, but do it knowing that I will *never* be your mate unless you honor our deal."

For a long while, he just stares at me, his eyes flicking between my own as though searching for something. Dissatisfied with whatever answer he finds, he releases me with a none too gentle flick of his wrist, then turns his back.

"We're done here."

Shaking my head derisively, I push back my chair.

The legs screech against the floorboards as I stand to face him. "No. We're far from done here, Killian. You and I both know this won't be over until one of us kills the other. So what are we waiting for? Why don't we just end this right now?"

He cocks his head just to the side as if considering my words. My heart thrashes with the possibility of fighting him again. In a way, us battling things out one last time could liberate me as much as it might destroy me. But it would be worth it, because this... whatever this thing is growing between us... that would die with him, or with me; whoever comes out victorious.

Either way, it will all be over.

Any and all feelings I harbor for him will be crushed before they have a chance to fully ripen and spread their venom.

That alone makes what I said worth it.

"As much as I'm sure you'd enjoy trying to kill me

again," he says at last, "I need you breathing for my plan to work. So if I were you, Zoriah, I'd start watching what poison you let escape that pretty little mouth of yours " He snaps his head forward again. "Fenrik! Get her out of my sight. I'm done with her."

The door swings open to reveal an awning shadow that swallows up the entryway. Fenrik's piercing eyes land on me and he flicks his chin to the side; a clear signal for me to go with him. Despite my reluctance to obey either of them, as I'm merely a frightened pup, I'd prefer to rot in a dungeon than spend another moment in Killian's presence.

It's with this in mind I adjust my blanket, trying vainly to hold onto a mere modicum of my dignity, and with my head held obnoxiously high, I make my way out. But it's his scathing huff that stops me.

I take a step back and stretch onto my tiptoes, bringing my lips to his ear. "When your body rots in an unmarked grave, Killian, and all of Arithym has forgotten you..." I lean closer, almost touching him, "then we will be done."

6

KILLIAN

Half of me wants to kill Zoriah Medley.

The other half wants to fuck the living daylights out of her.

I scowl as I pour a whisky and throw back the contents. The liquor burns down my throat and I close my eyes, savoring the sharp, bitter taste. The door opening announces my brother's arrival. By the way he lingers silently in the shadows, I know there's something on his mind and that whatever it is will likely piss me off.

"Spit it out," I growl, squeezing and rotating my neck.

Muscles crack as I let out a sigh. Gods, I need to shift. Or fuck. Anything that does not include me standing here breathing in Zoriah's lingering, intoxicating scent.

Why does she always smell like fucking violets?

Even when she nearly killed me and I lay bathed in my own blood, I could still smell her.

Still taste her.

"You can't keep her locked up forever, Alpha."

I open my eyes and turn my head just so in Fenrik's

direction. "Watch me. That female will remain locked up until she learns her place in my pack."

He slightly lowers his gaze. "And what place is that? The place of your mate or your prisoner?"

I slam my fist on the table. "That is her choice to make! I'm merely giving her a taste of both. Your job is to protect her—*not* parade her around in clothes that she has no fucking right to. You're lucky we're brothers, Fen, or I'd have ripped your throat out for what you did. Never defile my mother's memory like that again."

If Zoriah had stayed a moment longer, I would have taken my anger out on her by fucking her on the dining table. From the moment she got here, I wanted to tear my mom's dress off and then fuck my rage into Zoriah's body. I'd have claimed her as well as punished her, and my fucking gods how the Moon Goddess tested me this night. If I had lost control so early in the game, everything would've been messed up.

I need to break Zoriah first before I take her.

To do that, I need her begging for my cock by the time I take her. That's the only way to break a spirit as strong as hers.

Fenrik lowers his gaze, the vein in his temple pulsing. "Understood."

I sigh and take another drink. "Good. Keep an eye on the female. Tomorrow, we'll go hunting. Something tells me we both fucking need it."

My brother nods and wordlessly leaves the room. He closes the door with more force than usual. Seems like the female's even getting underneath his skin. Hmph. I pour another whiskey and slam it back, my pulse accelerating all over again. Who the fuck is Zoriah, anyway?

All I've been able to gather about her is that she possesses no living relatives and despises me with deep, burning passion. It's her hatred for me that hardens my cock every time she looks at me, making it nearly impossible to restrain myself around her. The urge to claim or torture her consumes every ounce of my being until all I can think about is her naked body spread over my altar.

Shit. At this rate, I might not be able to wait until the full moon.

I clench my hands at my side and grind my teeth, a growl building in the depth of my throat. Before I quite register it, I'm making my way to her with long, heavy strides.

Fenrik stands outside her cell. I dismiss him with a curt nod, wait until he closes the door, and then turn to the female crushed in the corner of her hell. The repugnant smell of decay and rodents invades my senses. I forgot how filthy this place is. Despite the fact I have enjoyed seeing light wolves rotting away in my dungeon many times before, the sight of Zoriah huddled in the corner, her head pressed to the bars, causes my stomach to heave in displeasure.

She opens her eyes at the sound of me unlocking the gate. "What do you want now, *Alpha*?"

Her derisive tone boils my blood more than it did earlier, and I fling the gate aside.

"I want you to tell me who you really are."

Her gaze widens. "You already know who I am."

I remove my shirt and prepare to shift with her. "No. The *real* you. Shift. Now."

I want to see if my wolf will react to her as strongly as my male side has. There's something about this female that gets under my skin in a way no one has ever been able to accomplish.

She gets to her feet, her body visibly tense. The pulse in her throat thrashes, drawing me closer until her heartbeat pounds in my ears like a subsonic drum.

"Shift, female."

The blood drains from her face as she wordlessly shakes her head. Defying my orders pisses me off at the best of times. With how hard my cock is, and how desperate I am to throw her against the wall and claim her, my patience is nonexistent. I stop in front of her, so close I could snap her pretty little neck if I wanted to. Her eyes latch onto me, wide and unblinking, causing a cruel smirk to twist my features.

"I. Said. S*hift*."

I growl the words out, a warning laced with malicious intent, but still she remains standing with an expression wiped clean of emotion. Shock, if anything. If she doesn't want to shift for me, I'll just have to make her.

And the best way to do that is to frighten her.

Or piss her off.

Based on our history, the latter will result in quicker results.

Still with the smirk on my face, I reach for her neck and unlock her collar with both hands. I place it into my pants and the female follows the movement with her eyes then travels over my exposed torso. She traces the tattoos slowly before meeting my gaze. Gently, I stroke the side of her face, and a shudder rakes through her.

"What's wrong, little mate? Why won't you shift?" I trail my thumb to the seam of her lips, brushing the pink flesh deliberately. "Scared your wolf will want to mate with me?"

That familiar crease forms between her eyebrows again. "No."

I slide my fingers around her neck and lightly squeeze where the collar had been not moments ago. For whatever reason, touching the female isn't bringing out the reaction I expected. Perhaps she's still processing the best way to respond. I am her captor, after all, but I can just as easily be her savior. Pissing me off might not be high on her list, if she knows what's good for her.

"Fighting me will get you nowhere," I whisper, caressing her. "So just give in. Submit to me. You know deep down you want to. I can see the desire in your eyes, little mate."

"I'm not..." The words catch in her throat. "I'm not your mate."

I grin at her. "*Yet*. How about I remedy that right now?"

Fear can accomplish wonderful, terrible things, and if frightening the female will result in her shifting, I'm not above doing it. Never claimed to be a good guy. In fact, I'm quite the fucking opposite. This one will soon know that.

"Stop doing this to me."

The female's plea is barely a whisper, but there's an undertone of desire that sends a jolt to my cock. Sliding my knuckle down the valley of her throat, I reach for the collar of her old dress. She must've thrown it back on when she got back here naked as the day she was born. I tear the material to her waist, exposing her bra. The lace clings to her porcelain skin, framing her tits in a way that's making it very fucking difficult not to bend down and bite them.

Shit!

Saliva pools in my mouth, and I swallow, the action more difficult than normal.

"One day, I'm going to kill you for good," she says.

I chuckle with dark amusement. "Oh, you will certainly try to, little mate." I cup her breast and trust in suppressed pleasure, tempting me to nibble it. "But what's that I smell, hm?"

A dark smile softens my features while a growl rumbles in the back of the female's throat.

"Your cunt getting wet for my cock again, that's what. Don't dare try to lie to me, Zoriah. I could smell your pussy ripening every goddamn time I looked at you. Fuck, I almost ate *you* for dessert, but then... then you had to go and run your pretty little mouth, didn't you?"

When I twist her nipple and dig my nail in, drawing blood, she lunges. The rest of her dress shreds to pieces as she transforms into her wolf. Flesh tears, bones crack, then there is the usual splitting noise seconds before the weight of her shifting pins me against the stone floor.

Beyond the wrinkled muzzle snarling in my face rests a pair of piercing blue eyes that cut through me like shards of ice. The crescent moon glowing on her temple is the last thing I expect to see, and my pulse spikes.

"So this is who you are," I say, reaching out slowly, "and why you've never submitted to me." Despite her warning snarl, I touch the birthmark, crooning quietly. "That's a good girl."

Her growl deepens as she narrows her eyes, but she doesn't bite me so that's a good sign. Not that I'd be unable to shift and fight her if I needed to. Something tells me I won't have to though.

"This is why they chose you as the offering, isn't it?" I ask, stroking her. "You're not only part dark wolf. You're an alpha."

She pulls her head back, enough for me to cease touching her. Instead, I search her blue eyes, so unlike the rest of her pack. Zoriah's cut through me like shards of sapphire sea glass. She's like a siren reeling me in and all thoughts of impending doom evade me as I'm pulled toward her.

All this time, I thought this female was my enemy, but she's as much a dark wolf as I am.

She even carries the Mark of Luna to boot. I don't think there's ever been a she-wolf alpha before. Could this be why Solas wanted to kill her?

For whatever fucking reason, I want to reach out again and pet her.

Claim her.

Dominate her.

She might be an alpha, but I'm *her* alpha, even if she does choose otherwise on the full moon. She'd be a fool to remain my prisoner though. I'll make her life ten times more unbearable than it is now.

"No matter what happens," I say, straightening into a less vulnerable position, "Solas will never touch you again. That I can promise."

The growl echoing in her chest quietens, and she stops snarling at me. It's at this moment she lowers her head and shifts back. No sooner does her naked form appear than she collapses into my arms. She crashes into a state of slumber that's common after a wolf's first shift. But surely the female has shifted before now?

Fuck. Is this why she wouldn't obey me?

Guilt threatens to snake into me.

She is still the enemy. Do not forget.

I slide my hands under her body and lift her up into my arms. Her head rolls limply against my chest. Zoriah is and always will be my enemy. But right now, she needs rest. She could be incapacitated for days.

I scan the dungeon for a place to lay her down.

Disgust twists my gut when I take in her pathetic bed. What was I thinking putting her in here? Well, that's just fucking it. I wasn't thinking. I was feeling so much rage and resentment that it blinded me from logic. She could've frozen in here. I shake my head with a grunt. Whether I like it or not, Zoriah is part dark wolf at the end of the day and should be given even the most basic rights of one. Tomorrow I will take her to one of the cabins. Fenrik will continue to guard her. Although she won't be quite free until she submits to me, she'll no longer live like an animal. It's the least I can do for one of my kin.

Even if they did try to kill me.

Twice.

I lay the assassin down on the blanket and move to turn away. Her hand catches my shirt, and I pause, staring down at her. Those flushed cheeks and half-opened lids, heavy with exhaustion, are dangerously tempting.

"I don't want to be sacrificed." Her voice is barely a croak.

"You won't. You're too useful an ally to me."

Her lips twitch, hinting at a smile. "Thought I was your prisoner?"

I arch a brow at her. "Who says you can't be both?"

She opens her lips to say something, but an alarm shrills in the background, immediately putting me on edge. Every muscle in my body tenses as wave after wave of hostile scents filter through my airways. I clench my jaw and lock the gate, ignoring the female's feeble efforts to stand or straighten into an upright position. In her defeat, she settles back down, and there's an uncharacteristic note of alarm on her face.

"What's going on?"

I hold her gaze, strangely fraught with an urge to comfort her. The fact that I'd want to comfort her at all results in enough anger to unleash my wolf and send him charging into battle.

"We're under attack."

7

ZORIAH

In spite of my weakened state, I muster what I can of my strength and drag myself off the floor. I cross the narrow length of the dungeon and shakily reach for the gate. My hands tremble but it's not from exhaustion anymore. It's from adrenaline. Seconds ago I was on the verge of passing out. Now I feel like I could run a marathon as an intense burst of energy tingles down my spine, regenerating my body.

Grasping the iron bars, I peer through them in search of any signs of life. Although I cannot see anyone in the near darkness, howls and battle cries fill the night air. Threaded amongst them is the distinctive smell of light fae. Not again. Their attack, however, gives me a moment of staggering clarity.

I'm alone.

Completely and utterly alone.

There's no grumpy beta standing outside my dungeon. No alphas playing tricks with my mind and body.

It's just me, and standing in the way of my freedom are iron bars.

A sudden urge to escape consumes me. An attack on the compound is a perfect opportunity to escape. If I could just reach the trees, I'll be able to make my way to a river and swim through it to mask my scent. From there, I'm not entirely sure, but anything is better than being held prisoner while my best friend suffers.

I can't just sit in this dungeon while Tristen endures goddess knows what, so I grab the bars and pull. The wrought-iron shrieks as I yank them apart, and to my astonishment, they bend. Enough for me to squeeze through them.

More screams and snarls echo outside, causing a shudder to rake through my body. I tiptoe down the dimly lit corridor. The wooden door at the end has either been left open or broken. Judging by the part of the door that's hanging off the hinges, I'm going to go with the latter.

Looks like someone tried to get through.

I take a deep breath and my stomach heaves at the scent cloying the air.

It is Solas.

Or at least, the light fae mercenaries hired by him. I'll never understand why anyone would want to do that let alone fae capable of shifting into wolves. Then again, Solas had me convinced he would be a good mate for me and that I was special to him. A derisive scoff escapes me, more out of nerves from the situation than anything. He's the most manipulative creature to ever walk the realm.

I gently open the door and peek out into the open. Dark wolves wrestle light fae wolves to the ground while a fire has been lit near the temple. Its orange flames stretch toward the inky-black sky like a fire demon. It's utter chaos around me, but this may be my only chance to escape.

Now that I can shift, I can save Tristan myself.

I don't need an alpha for help anymore. I *am* one. My strength in wolf form should be able to rival that of Solas.' I could even challenge him for the place of alpha. I'd become the Light Alpha, and Killian and I would once again be enemies.

It's worth a shot, if not for revenge, at least for rescuing Tristan.

Taking a tentative step forward, I search both ways before hurrying across the clearing. Wolves and people run around me, some attacking while others seek shelter in the temple. Even some of the scattering livestock scramble after them. I hope none of them get injured. I make a break for the trees but the fire that spread to one of the cabins collapses on the ground, blocking my path. Through all the smoke and wisps of ash distorting my vision, it's nearly impossible to see anything. But I've got to find another way into the forest before anyone catches me.

I pivot and there, across the way, Killian's wolf lunges.

An almost horrifying awe grips hold of me.

I root to the spot, watching as he effortlessly rips a grey wolf's throat out with his blood-stained fangs. He then tears his way through enemy after enemy with ruthless, malicious ease. His fur is darker, even when the moonlight catches him, and I realize it's because he's bathed in so much blood. I've seen him hunt and fight before but not like this.

He's utterly barbaric.

Animalistic.

This is precisely what separates them from us.

However, right now, I'm rooting for them. This is their territory the fae wolves attacked and I've got a dreadful feeling it's because of me. My gaze lands on a pathway cutting through the trees. I rush toward it, but then I stop when an ear-splitting cry splits through my mind.

"No, please! Please don't hurt me!"

An icy chill sweeps through me.

I spin around in circles in search of her, and my stomach churns when two white wolves corner her against a wall. She's trapped with nowhere to go, her little terrified face streaked in tears, then she ducks underneath them and runs.

Instincts kick in, and my wolf side takes over.

My paws hit the ground running as I charge after the wolves. It's incredible how at ease I am with her. Letting my wolf take over feels as natural to me as breathing and I can't imagine not being able to do this anymore. All it took was for Killian to trigger me, and now I'm whole again. She's an extension of my flesh and bone; without her, I'd be empty.

It feels incredible.

The girl's scent leads me to a graveyard behind the temple. The fire from the building casts an auburn glow over the headstones and the group of fae wolves now cornering the girl from before. Every protective instinct I possess lunges me into action. Bones crunch and flesh tears beneath my fangs.

My wolf is twice the size of these males, and I know how powerful they are. I've seen them fight. However, as I tear through them and discard their bodies without a flicker of remorse, I realize something staggering: freedom pales in comparison to revenge.

It also tastes so much sweeter on my tongue.

I lick the blood from my lips and let out a low, warning snarl to the faewolf eyeing me across the graveyard. The wolf lowers his head and retreats, not before an axe nearly cuts through his skull. Goddess, that would've been amazing. The blade slams into a tree and Fenrik appears not a moment later, yanking it out with a hand dripping in fresh blood.

He catches me guarding and there's a fleeting look of surprise on his face. Maybe he thought I'd have escaped by now. I almost did. His surprise is swiftly overridden by a ferocious mask of fury when he notices the girl.

A quiet yip draws my attention back to her. She's shifted into a tiny, shivering pup covered in dark brown fur with white spots on her tail. Thank *Nuala* I reached her in time.

Bending down, I gently take her by the scruff of the neck. Branches shrouded in fire snap and fall down around us when I return to the heart of the chaos. I don't stop though and continue running until I find a place to hide her.

As soon as I do, a fae wolf charges for me and our claws meet in a fury of rage.

The surge of maternal instincts has heightened my bloodlust in a way I never thought myself capable of. Is this what Killian meant? Did he know all along how blissfully feral I would become once I finally shifted? Throwing a knife and arrow to his throat doesn't quite compare to the way I'm tearing through these fae wolves in order to protect the pup.

When the battle is over and the dark wolves win, a deadly silence drapes over the land. All the while, I guard the girl and snarl at anyone who comes near, including her own kin. I won't leave until I've returned her home safely.

It's only at the sight of her crawling out from underneath me do I move.

She jumps excitedly as though her life hadn't just been

on the line. "That was so amazing! You totally kicked their butt!"

The glee on her face reminds me of a time when I was young and Maya would tell tales of how Airthym came to be. It's strange, now, to think everything was created in perfect harmony to balance each other. When the gods plucked their hearts out and placed them high above the realms, they created night and day, and from those came the dark fae and the light fae. It was the fae who created the first ever shifters. Originally, we were intended to be guardians of the sun and moon but war changed that. Now, all wolves care about is being superior and claiming the rest of Drokadis as their own.

So much for balance.

A light tap on the side of my head brings me back to the present. I nudge the girl's small hand and allow her to stroke me. Her eyes widen into orbs when she takes in my glowing birthmark.

"Wooow. You... You are like Alpha Killian. You are an alpha!"

Her exclamation echoes around the clearing, drawing more attention to us. With the chaos now over, many of the dark wolves have shifted back, some of them more injured than others. As each of them take in my wolf form, for the first time since I was brought here, they look at me as the predator, not the prey, in which I am.

And my wolf relishes their reaction.

I hold myself tall, my head lifted high, and the glow from my crescent moon sheds a halo of sapphire light on the ground around me. A dead grey wolf lies by my blood-stained paws. The girl steps over the corpse as though it's an everyday thing for her.

"I go home now," she says, nodding decidedly. "Goodbye!"

She makes an effort to run away, but I halt her with a light tug on her sleeve. I don't want her walking around unattended. At least not until I know she's safe.

The girl beams and stands back so she can lower herself. "Okay, you come with me. I can show you my rocks. Do you like rocks? I have a whole jar filled with them." She climbs up and gently holds on to her neck. "Papa says the one under my pillow was blessed by the Moon God Himself and it keeps my nightmares away. Do you get nightmares? I'm Freya, by the way."

I shake my head in reply, my lips lifting in a smile. She probably knows my name by now.

Lowering myself so that Freya can climb on top of me, I trace her scent back to a familiar little cabin. This is where Vincent healed me—where Killian dragged me from my bed and then into the Temple of Ryviel. It's the healer's den.

Could Vincent be her dad?

Tentatively, I approach the steps and Freya quickly slides off. The instant her boots touch the ground, the splintered door slams open and a highly panicked Vincent rushes to meet her.

"Freya!"

She runs into the male's arms, and he squeezes her as though she's the most precious thing in the world. I imagine to him that she is. I've always hoped that my parents thought the same about me when they were alive.

A stab of longing spears me, as it always does, followed by an all too familiar rage that grips me at thought of their deaths. I push the memory to the back of my mind and stand back, watching the sweet reunion.

Vincent sets her down, and his eyes slowly land on my

face. He doesn't say anything, only nods in a way that instantly conveys his gratitude. I incline my head, too, and then turn around. Fenrik stands watching me, one hand clutching a gun, the other my broken collar.

His choice is clear: death or imprisonment.

For a fleeting moment, I consider challenging him and fighting for my freedom. But as I look around at the dead bodies—only some of them dark wolves—an urge to help them grips hold of me. Staying here could mean Solas will never again be able to shift. He'll always be weaker than his enemy, and sooner or later, the Strays will cease their alliance with him. I don't imagine the rogue wolves will want to make a treaty with an alpha who cannot even shift. Plus, it's clear I have a greater chance of staying alive if there's more shifted wolves around me. I could try to free Tristan myself, but if I die, he dies too. It'll all be for nothing.

Maybe I am better off staying here.

"Let's get going, Medley."

The beta's deep voice drags me from my stupor.

An intense exhaustion rakes through me and my paws tremble on the surface. Even if I did choose to run, I don't think my legs could take me very far. The adrenalin from the battle has all but drained my body, leaving me exhausted and my bones sore all over.

I shift back, and just like the previous time, I collapse under my own weight. Killian isn't here to catch me this time, but his beta is. He lifts me and drapes my arm over his shoulder.

He's quiet during the short journey to my cell, probably wondering why the hell I chose to stay. When he leads me away from the dungeon, a sudden unease grips me. This is the path we took when I was summoned to eat with Killian.

"Where're we going?"

Fenrik glances at me, then continues up the familiar winding path. He doesn't provide an answer, but by the time we reach Killian's quarters, there's no need to. I yank my arm back and try to push away. Fenrik grabs my arm and wordlessly opens the door, then he takes me inside. The room, however, remains bereft of the alpha's presence. I don't let my relief show though.

"And where is his Royal Highness?" I ask.

Fenrik enters the room with me but lingers in the doorway. "Paying his respects."

As an alpha it makes sense. What doesn't make sense is why I've been brought here.

I march over to the leather sofa and drop down onto the middle. "So I get to sit with you? Great. You're a fantastic conversationalist."

I snort at my own joke because I'm lucky if I get more than a few words out of this male. He leans against the door frame and stares at me. Either I'm too annoyed or tired to care, but I hold his gaze.

His stony expression is, as always, void of emotion.

Damn he's good at keeping a straight face.

He'd actually be handsome if he cracked a smile once in a while. Doesn't really seem like his kind of style though. Fenrik always looks like he wants to either kill me or eat me for supper. Both options are definitely not on my to-do list.

"So...," I say in an effort to fill the silence. Because this isn't awkward at all. "Quite nice weather we had tonight, all things considered."

"Why did you choose to stay?" The beta's abrupt question takes me momentarily off guard. "You had the chance to escape," he adds quietly yet firmly, "but you didn't. You fought with us, for us. Why?"

I glance down at my torn dress, as if the tears in the beautiful fabric hold an answer to the question. But all that comes to me is the truth.

"Because a little girl needed my help." I lift my gaze and look hard at him. "Because regardless of which pack we come from—light, dark, whatever else is out there—when you see someone in need of help, you freaking help them. I couldn't just stand and watch her die."

He scrutinizes me for a moment and then nods. "The alpha will be here soon. Do you need a healer?"

I shake my head. "No. Do I need a gun to protect myself from the alpha?"

The beta smirks at that. "No. Besides, I've seen the way you fight. Not bad for a first-time shifter."

He leaves before I can ask how he knew that.

Did he catch me shifting in the dungeon?

The door closes softly in his wake, but the beta's scent lingers on the opposite side, telling me he's still close by so he can keep watch. There's a hint of burning leaves in his scent which is oddly familiar, but I can't quite seem to place it.

Of course he'd continue standing guard outside, though.

Even if I did choose to stay here of my own volition, I'm still just his alpha's prisoner at the end of the day. We'll always be enemies, but I might not always be his captive. Not if I choose differently on the full moon. Then I would be Killian's mate—bonded forever to the alpha who killed my parents—but there's no coming back from that.

Not ever.

8

ZORIAH

Water trickles down my face and I blink awake, instantly aware I've fallen asleep in the last place I'd ever want to.

Killian's room.

"Hello there, pup. Sleep well?"

I shoot up into a sitting position and glare at Killian. He smirks at me and takes a swig from his bottle of whiskey and it takes everything in me not to reach out and kick the bottle from his hand.

"Thought I told you to stay in your cage?"

"You mean that delightful, cozy room with the huge bed?" I wipe the droplets of whiskey from my face and scowl at him. "Yeah, when the threat of impending doom kicked in, I decided I'd much rather die amongst wolves than the rats scuttling about your precious little hellhole."

He leans in slightly, enough that I'm forced to breathe in his overwhelming scent. Mingled with the whisky and the blood staining his ripped clothes, his scent invades my senses like a blanket of darkness, consuming everything. There's an undercurrent of something that reminds me of a distant memory I can't seem to quite reach. It's there, right in front of me, but I can't touch it.

"You don't know the meaning of hell, sweetheart."

My lips tilt in a smirk. "Really? Because I'm looking at the devil right now, and I'm not done with him yet."

He mirrors my smirk, but there's a distinct cruelty in it that sends a shiver through me. He punctures his lower lip with his teeth, drags it back and forth, then leans back.

"So," he drawls, dragging a hand through his hair. "You ready to tell me your story yet, little mate?"

I scrunch my nose in disgust. "What story? And stop calling me that."

Little lamb. Little mate. I don't want to be anyone's little anything.

I'd rather Killian called me his prisoner than his 'little mate.'

He takes another drink, a long one. "I'll call you whatever the fuck I want, she-wolf. You're not the alpha here."

This motherfucking —

I catch the words from slipping off my tongue and school my features.

"True," I say instead, "but I am an alpha. And part dark wolf, according to you."

His eyes darken a shade deeper. "Not according to me. According to the birthmark. So, are you gonna tell me who betrayed my pack and bred with a light wolf, or should I start interrogating every dark wolf out there until I find the culprit? I ain't above doing both."

I glare at him with sheer and utter dispassion. "Are you fucking serious?"

He laughs like this is all a big joke to him.

As if he never tortured my parents and let them bleed

out in the snow, leaving two pups to fend for themselves. Tristan and I almost died because of him.

I often wished I had when I was younger and riddled with survivor's guilt.

Killian props a leg on the edge of the sofa and stares at me. "One thing you should know about me, *little mate,* is that when it comes to my pack, I'm always fucking serious. Now tell me who the rat is so I can go pay them a little visit."

Tears of rage threaten my eyes. This is the wolf who murdered my parents in cold blood. This is the wolf who's blackmailing me into becoming his mate. This is the wolf I have longed my entire life to put an end to. All the emotions I've suppressed since coming here come surging to the surface, and I jump off the sofa.

"*You*! You betrayed *us*!"

The male just looks at me curiously, almost in amusement, which heightens my fury. There's not a flicker of remorse on his face—nothing other than his usual smug expression.

"Do you truly regret nothing about killing them?"

He doesn't even blink. "I've killed a lot of people and each of them deserved it. You're gonna have to be more specific, sweetheart. Who have I supposedly killed now?"

The words catch in my throat like razors. "My parents!"

His dark brows rise slightly, and his muscles tense. He tries to mask it by removing his leg from the sofa and straightening to his full height, probably to intimidate me, but I catch the pulse thrashing in his throat. I've always been good at noticing the small tell-tales others try so hard to hide. Killian's is the way he clenches his jaw to such a degree that he pops the vein on his temple.

He cocks his head, his forehead creasing. "When was this?"

"Twenty-one years ago, by the Wyvern's Tavern. You slaughtered my mom and dad like butchered lambs then left me and Tristan to die out in the snow. We would've frozen to death come morning if Solas hadn't found us." A disgusted snarl stretches over my lips. "Rule number one of being a light wolf: always cover your tracks, especially when there's blood involved. You would've saved yourself a whole lot of hassle if you'd just finished me then and there."

He stares at me in amazement. "You think I killed your parents and that's why you've spent all these years hunting me? So you could avenge them?"

"I don't *think* you killed them. I know you did it!"

He scoffs, and oh my sweet fuck, it takes every ounce of willpower in me not to punch him in the throat.

"Did you see me do it?"

The question catches me off guard, and I scowl at my hesitation.

"No," I grit out.

"I see. Did this—Tristan, right?—did he see me do it?"

I bite my tongue, refusing to give him the satisfaction of another negative answer. After all, the only people who witnessed my parents' deaths were Solas and his sister, Maya. Our sweet healer never did tell me what happened. All she said was that she found me and Tristan in a pool of blood by the creek and that Solas went after the Dark Alpha, but never found him. Since then they'd been at war with each other.

"I'm going to take your silence as a no." Killian sighs and rubs his neck, drawing my attention to the scar I left there. The only time I ever came close to killing him. "Then tell me, who did witness this slaughter you speak of? Solas? The alpha who groomed you to be his sacrifice?"

I tense my body at the derision implied in his voice. Solas was the one who found us that day. Could... could he have lied about my parents' death because he was the one who murdered them? His deceit is hardly difficult to believe since he did try sacrificing me. His whole pack lied for him and had me convinced I was going to be his mate.

The corner of his lips quirk. "Looks like you've already found your answer."

I snap my head up and glare at him. "Even if it's true, I would never take your word for it. You're still just a monster at the end of the day who's killed hundreds of shifters."

His smirk vanishes like snow melting beneath the sun. "I might be a monster in your eyes, but I've never killed the undeserving and certainly not a fucking woman. Even wolves like me have a code to live by."

"And what code is that? To maim, steal, and kill?" I snarl at him. "Because that's what wolves like you are known for."

In one powerfully swift movement, he grabs me by the throat and pins my back to the wall. "You might be an alpha but you're in *my* pack now, and you better start showing me some goddamn fucking respect!"

"Or else— what?" I ask between gasps of air. "You'll— kill— me? Solas— will— thank you for it. What are you— waiting for?"

Reality dawns on him and he slackens his grip on my neck. My pulse thrashes against his fingers as he maintains his close proximity, his enormous shadow swallowing up my own. Along with his fury is an intense hunger burning in his eyes that threatens to weaken me in his grasp. It pools from his body into my own and spreads through me like a cloak of forbidden desire.

It's not only forbidden but unwanted.

Yet, as his racing heartbeat dances in sync with my own, his scent wraps around me and clouds my mind, turning my thoughts of revenge into nothing more than an unquenchable thirst for pleasure. His growl fans my cheeks as he adds pressure to my throat, cutting off a little of my air supply.

"You'll die when I say you can die. You got that, little mate?"

Without waiting for a reply, Killian crushes his lips to mine with a deep, ferocious hunger that seizes the very air from my lungs and holds it prisoner just like the rest of me.

Only this time, I surrender to him willingly.

9

ZORIAH

Killian throws me onto the bed and licks the side of my neck.

"The next time I mount you, Zoriah, we'll be mates," he whispers, running his fangs over the shell of my ear. He bites down hard, causing me to gasp. "Not a day will go by when your cunt isn't filled with my cum."

I strain my neck to frown at him. "Only if I choose to be. I haven't made my decision yet."

He chuckles. "Oh, you will choose to be my mate, sweet pet." Then he flips me over onto my stomach and presses my face into the pillow. "You already want me to claim you. Just look at how well you're presented, waiting to be mounted like the good little bitch in heat you are. You're practically begging to be taken, and since I'd hate to disappoint you..."

He groans as he enters me. There's no warning, no preamble, only raw, carnal fucking and his heavy grunts echoing my own. The fact that he called me his bitch should infuriate me to no end, but my reply is but a stifled moan that is forcefully buried in the sheets.

Stars paint my vision as Killian seizes my throat and pushes me harder into the bed. Any moans that escape me now are muffled by the silk bedding, and all I can focus on is how roughly he's taking me and how much I'm enjoying it.

Half an hour ago, I wanted to kill this alpha.

Now I'm letting him take me without putting up a fight.

If this is what he wants, I'll give him it, and then I'll finally get what I want.

Tristan.

Killian's heavy breaths trickle down my neck, causing me to convulse from pleasure.

"You're where you belong now, little mate." He thrusts even harder. "Right here"—deeper—"with your cunt"—another thrust—"wrapped around my cock." He moans when I squeeze around him and then he slaps my ass. "Aaaah, fuck, just like that."

I do it again, and his moan turns into a deep, primal growl in which my own wolf answers to. She howls inside of me, pacing frantically like a starved beast, and calls out to Killian's wolf in a way I've never experienced until now. It's as if she's been asleep all these years only to be roused by Killian's ruthless mating.

Except, this isn't mating.

This is two enemies fucking their hatred into each other's bodies.

As Killian roughly takes me from behind, I push back equally as powerfully, fueled by all the years I've spent hunting and hating him. He lets go of my waist to steady himself on the headboard, but I grab him and dig my fingernails into his skin. Blood permeates the air, and he snarls, tightening his hand on my throat in warning.

I continue to claw at him.

I squeeze around his thick cock with each perfectly timed thrust, knowing full well he enjoys me clenching him as much as he detests me drawing his blood. But I want to hurt him. I want to taste Killian's blood on my tongue and then spit it in his face.

As though I uttered my desire out loud, Killian frees his hand with an effortless yank and smears his blood over my lips. Every nerve in my body tingles the instant I taste him. Instead of the sharp, copper tang I prepare myself for, the alpha's blood is sweet and addicting.

Intoxicating.

I cease moving and slide my tongue over wounds I created with my bare hands. Every droplet that lands on my tongue is even more delicious and addictive than the last.

How is this even possible? His blood should taste bitter and disgusting. Unless...

Taking my gasp for a protest, Killian pulls back and threads a hand in my hair, tilting me so I'm looking at him. There's a playful gleam in his eyes I've never seen before. He smirks at me.

"Patience, little mate. You'll get more of my blood when I claim you." He drives into me again, hard and fast. "Tell me that's what you want, Zoriah."

"N-no..." The word leaves me brokenly but it's directed at him. "I can't... this can't be..."

This can't be happening!

But there's no other explanation I know of, which means it is happening.

The reason Killian's blood tastes so amazing, that I crave it at all, is because my wolf has chosen him.

She wants to mate with Killian.

More devastating is the fact that deep down, I wanted her to, and that revelation shatters me to the depths of my core. Screams of pain-filled ecstasy rip their way from my throat, and Killian smothers them with his lips. He spears my mouth with his tongue and turns my cries into moans of pleasure that cause the rest of me to convulse in orgasm.

He swallows my sounds with a groan of his own, then wraps a hand around my throat. He holds me down while he chases his release, his thrusts rapid, hungry, almost animalistic. He grabs the headboard and nearly shatters the wood when he spills inside me with a deafening roar. His weight pressing down against me demonstrates the sheer power of his body, and for a moment, he just stays there, his breaths heavy, his cock pulsing inside of me. Then he falls to my side and the two of us lie panting together. Surely, now that I've submitted to him, he'll start fulfilling his end of the bargain.

Otherwise, I have nothing else to give him.

Nothing more to entice him with.

I tilt my head, and Killian's black, impenetrable eyes pour through me. "Now that you've got what you wanted, will you go for Tristan? Tonight?"

The alpha throws his legs over the bed and pulls on his pants with rough, jerky movements. The fact that his knuckles are blanched from clenching his fingers so hard tell me this is not the kind of after-sex conversation he wanted to have with me.

"Already thinking of your lover boy, eh? Seems I didn't fuck you hard enough then." He throws back his head and shouts at the ceiling: "Fenrik, get fucking in here. Now!"

The door opens not a second later, and Fenrik enters the room. His usually impassive features are shadowed by a dark emotion I'm unable to fully decipher. The harsh lines drawn around his narrowed eyes are unusual and make him look like he hasn't slept in days. Although they fleetingly sweep over me before landing on Killian's back, the silent revulsion in his gaze was palpable enough to elicit feelings of shame in me. I pull the sheet up to my neck, a vain effort to hide my embarrassment, but the heat rushing to my cheeks gives me away. Damn it.

Killian pushes off the bed and reaches for his belt. "Take her back. I'm done with her."

There's those words again. *Done with me.* Although this time it's different because this time it's personal; a cruel disregard of me as anything other than a body to gratify himself with, and I let it happen.

How could I?

I drop the sheet as an intense need to wash his scent off quickly consumes me. The bloodstain of my surrendered innocence glares back at me, a poignant reminder of the severity of my actions.

Why did I let this happen?

Killian is the one who wants to claim me as his mate—not the other way around. He made it perfectly clear he wanted my body in return for his help, so I gave him that in hopes it would speed up Tristan's rescue. It didn't. My sacrifice was all for nothing.

I never wanted any of this.

By all accounts, I shouldn't be surprised by his reaction, but the rage that burns through me is so much stronger because of all the passion we shared mere moments ago.

I focus my anger on the beta, hoping to strike Killian where I know it hurts him most.

His stupid pride.

"What about you, Fenrik?" I give the wolf my sweetest, most seductive smile. "Are you done with me, too, or should we pick up where your alpha left off? Goddess knows I'm ready."

I glance at Killian from the corner of my eyes. Nothing at first. The male doesn't so much as look at me, but then his back muscles tense and his knuckles blanch as he grips the belt half-looped through his pants.

"Just take her back," he growls, fastening himself.

I glare at his back. The alpha's lack of reaction angers me more than if he had lashed out. I mean, I just insulted him in front of his beta, and he's acting like he couldn't care less. Maybe he wouldn't care if I slept with Fenrik, and maybe I should just to piss him off.

However, the thought of risking Tristan's life just to piss Killian off holds me in check. Tristan needs me, and I need to bite my tongue. At least for now.

Despite the blush assaulting my cheeks, I reach for my dress with my head held obnoxiously high. Both males watch unashamedly as I slide the material over my body and then throw my legs over the bed. I despise this dress more than Killian's scent poisoning my body, but marching butt naked through hostile territory is hardly an appealing option right now.

Even if spitting at Killian would make my day.

Hell, my whole year.

With Tristan at the forefront of my mind, I make my way peacefully to the door. Fenrik holds it open, but I pause to glance back at the alpha. He's moved to the window where he gazes pensively over his domain. Every inch of him screams alpha, from the incredible, well-defined muscles sculpting his entire body to the dominant way in which he holds himself, yet how he just treated me is nothing short of cowardly.

"You are a coward," I say to his back, "and unworthy to be my mate. There's your answer."

Without a backward glance, I leave the alpha to stew in his enraged silence.

The one thing Killian could do that *might* make me forgive him is if he saved Tristan. But he's too much of a coward to do it. That's why he's dragging this on and keeping me here. He speaks of revenge and defeating Solas, and yet here I am, the very key to achieving his goal—the piece to win the game—but he would rather have me locked up in a safe.

Or in this instance, a cage.

At least you protect valuables in a safe.

Here, I'm just an object to be used whenever and however her captor pleases.

And tonight I let it happen willingly.

I need to find a way out of here before the full moon rises.

The walk to the dungeon is tense and silent. I don't really have anything to say to the beta. I do hope he doesn't take me up on the offer I joked about in Killian's room. It's not that Fenrik isn't attractive—far from it. It's that there's only so much of my light I'm willing to surrender before I turn into a dark wolf just like them.

The thought has me anchoring my feet to the ground, and I stare blankly ahead without really seeing anything around me. It's as if reality has fully dawned on me and with a cruel, cold snarl reminds me of what I just did: I slept with Killian. I gave myself to the one alpha I've despised for as long as I can remember, but in the end, it didn't even matter. Killian still refuses to help me before time runs out and that's if it hasn't done so already.

A gut-wrenching feeling cuts through me, causing my skin to crawl and my stomach to heave. Suddenly, I'm standing in the middle of my dungeon and the walls are closing in. My lungs clamp shut as the ground beneath my feet trembles as though the world itself is being ripped apart and my lungs refuse to take in any air.

What have I done? What have I done?!

I came to the Shadowlands for revenge, but the only one I'm destroying is myself.

"What're you waiting for?"

Fenrik's voice registers in my mind, yet I'm unable to respond.

"Look at me," he orders, seizing me roughly by the shoulders. "Look at me, damn it."

His features are a watery haze as tears burn my eyes and distort my vision. With surprising, and unexpected, tenderness he lifts my chin to search my eyes with his blue ones.

"What have I done?" I whisper out loud, my saliva catching in my throat like razor blades.

"I let this happen. I did it all willingly."

Fenrik shrugs. "You chose to survive, is all, and sometimes survival takes sacrifice. Real fucking sacrifice, the kind some folks just aren't willing to make. That's what separates the ones who adapt"—he lightly taps my forehead—"you and me, from those who die. It's just the nature of the game out there."

The poignancy of his words brings more tears to my eyes. It's the most Fenrik has ever said to me. Nevertheless, even if there is truth to be found in his words, what I did back there with Killian wasn't self-preservation. It was a moment of weakness in which I used my body to get what I wanted, only to fail and be rejected afterward. My heart rate soars again, and I close my eyes, as though trying to banish the memory from my mind. Fenrik gently taking my chin forces me to open them again, and I peer up at him through my wet lashes. His handsome face twists into a grimace that sends a chill through me.

"Get the hell out of your head, Medley, and keep those eyes on me. Don't you look away now." His own voice drops into a whisper, a gentle caress of air against my burning skin. "Now breathe. That's it."

I take a shuddering breath in through my nose and release it from my mouth. Pressed so closely together, all I can smell and breathe in is Fenrik's scent. It wraps round me like a warm blanket, the smell akin to leaves kindling over hot coals.

Burning leaves...

"It was you," I murmur, wiping the tears from my eyes. "You brought me that blanket, didn't you? But... why?"

He shrugs like it meant nothing. "Figured you could use one. Besides, if you get sick, it's me who has to take care of your sorry ass, and you're already a pain in *my* ass as it is."

I blink up at him. *Take care?* "More like imprison, you mean."

His dark eyes turn into slits. "Take care. Guard. Protect. You've seen the way the others look at you, waiting to rip your throat out. Even with the alpha's orders to stay away, you being here is like taking a piss on our fallen. You remember little Freya?"

The girl I saved yesterday.

"Of course I do," I say.

"Well, she had a big sister. Wasn't much older than Freya is now." The male pauses and a dark expression shadows him. I swallow the lump in my throat but the saliva struggles to go down. Something tells me this story isn't going to be a pleasant one. "She was mutilated by a light wolf after straying over the border. The bastard found her before we did, and he..."

Fenrik trails off, the muscles on his jaw clenching.

I probe him quietly. "What happened to her?"

He huffs and contorts his features in disgust, then he shakes his head. "Forget it. Just know that your kind will never be welcome here, even if you did become their alpha's mate. They'll never accept you."

This I already know. It's not like the dark wolves have been subtle about their dislike for me. I doubt any of them would ever learn to accept me. They'd simply tolerate me as their alpha's mate, nothing more, and Fenrik may be right; even then, they might also still try to kill me. I know more than anyone how intense the longing is to kill the one you hate.

"I don't want to be welcome here, anyway," I say, "and I hope to the goddess that monster who killed Freya's sister got what he deserved."

Fenrik scoffs as he releases me. "Oh, he did, and more. Alpha and I made damn sure of it." The wolf crosses his arms and looks hard at me. "My point is, you're never going to get what you want by staying. Captive, mate—it doesn't fucking matter here. Killian won't get your friend until he's absolutely certain it will guarantee Solas' death. Going by how long his plan of attack is taking, you could be waiting weeks for it to happen."

I tense at the word. *Weeks*? Tristan might not survive another day for all I know. That's if he's still alive, but right now that's the only outcome I'm willing to consider.

"Then what are you suggesting?" I ask.

He stares at me unwaveringly. "We make a deal. A new one, just between us."

I stare at him in disbelief. "I don't think deal means what the wolves around here think it means. Just look at

Killian. Even you said he might never fulfil his end of the bargain, so why should I make a deal with you?"

Fenrik looks me dead in the eye, his gaze filled with unwavering determination. "Because Killian is a fool and I am not."

I gasp with blatantly feigned horror. "But Fenrik, that's your beloved alpha you're speaking of!"

Something dark flashes in his eyes. "Like I said, he's a fool. A fool to give you all this time to make a damn decision. I know what I want, and I'm not waiting around for it."

Well, that is true. Fenrik definitely seems like the kind of wolf to go straight for the kill instead of letting it bleed out. Waste not want not, this guy doesn't beat around the bush.

"Say we did make a deal... What do you get out of it?"

He doesn't blink or hesitate. "To become an alpha. The only way I can do that is by mating with another alpha, and as handsome as I look, I don't bat for Killian's team if you get my drift. I want an alpha she-wolf." His pupils dilate, blown with an unspoken lust that makes my heart skip a beat. "I want you, Zoriah."

I stare at him in disbelief. "You want me?"

But why the hell would he want me?

"You," he repeats with a nod. "And you want your best friend rescued and the Light Alpha dead. I can do that for you. Tonight."

My disbelief turns into confusion. Why the hell would he risk abandoning his pack just to become an alpha? Couldn't he just challenge Killian, and if he won, take over the Shadowlands?

"Why do you even want to become an alpha?" I ask.

He pauses as if debating whether to answer. "I want to

start my own pack, one that isn't divided by light and darkness."

"So pack where all wolves will be accepted?"

"That's the plan."

"But... don't you hate my kind, too?"

He shakes his head. "Nah. Not as much as the others. My sister's part light wolf, on my mom's side, and I'd do anything to protect her. Haven't seen her since she was a pup though. Heard she's got a litter of her own now. I bet they're just as stubborn as she was." He smiles fondly as though stumbling upon a memory that had since been forgotten. "She's a bit like you, actually. Bull-headed. Never gives up. Loyal to a fault."

This is exactly how I would describe the Maya who raised me, especially the part about her loyalty. There's nothing she wouldn't do to protect her family. She almost let Solas kill me just to save them. I peer into Fenrik's face and my breath hitches. His eyes. I can't believe I never noticed how similar they are to Maya's. They're the same shade of periwinkle, similar hooded lids, and they even have the same long, blond lashes framing them.

"You have the same eyes," I say, leaning back. Then it hits me. "Wait. That means Solas is your half-brother, too?"

His upper lip curls back. "He has the same father as Maya but different mothers. I'd sooner slit my throat if I were related to that son of a bitch."

I smile at that. "Then we have something in common, don't we?"

He nods. Once. "That we do. The only difference between me and Killian is that I don't fuck around. You want your friend back? We'll get him out tonight." Before I can reply, he says in a dangerously possessive tone: "But know that if you come with me, you're coming as my mate, not my prisoner. That's the deal."

I take a deep breath and consider my options. While the prospect of making another deal with a dark wolf isn't ideal, this is by far the most tempting one. It offers not only Tristan's immediate freedom, but also the chance to start a pack that could unite our species. Perhaps even put an end to the war and blood sacrifices once and for all.

As slightly intimidating as Fenrik is, there's something about him that does not put me on edge like his alpha. Even now, as he regards me in patient silence, waiting for my answer, I'm not afraid or angered by him. There's only one answer I can give him and it rolls off my tongue before I can catch it.

"I'll do it."

"Then I'll come for you tonight. Be ready."

He leaves without a backward glance, his fading footsteps echoing down the hallway outside. I've been ready to leave this hell the moment I entered its gates.

It's time to get the fuck out of here.

10
ZORIAH

I t's midnight when he arrives.

He opens the gate and tosses me a backpack. "Hurry up. We don't have a lot of time. The feast is almost over."

I nod and open the backpack with quick, slightly trembling fingers. The dark wolves have been celebrating since dusk and they're growing restless outside. I've lost count of the number of times a fight has broken out and someone has been slammed against the dungeon wall.

I lay the clothes out on the floor—a pair of black pants, a short-sleeved gray t-shirt, and some boots. Last to be pulled from the bag is a thick chain of unusually shaped flowers. The silver petals smell like lavender and curve inward like a crescent moon. A similar chain hangs around Fenrik's neck. Once I'm dressed, I drape mine there too and run a hand down my pants with a relieved sigh.

It feels so good to wear proper clothes again.

"What's with the flowers?" I ask, bruising my fingertips over them. "I've never seen these in Drokadis before."

"That's because they don't grow here. Munelites are

native to the mountains of Mythris. Wearing them after battle is a tradition all dark creatures honor in memory of our fallen." He lifts a single petal. "This alone is strong enough to mask your scent. It'll help you the border undetected."

"Got it. How long until we get there?"

I was barely alive the last time I crossed the border. All I can remember is how beautiful the glowing river had been when I crossed it into the Shadowlands. The rest of the journey is just a haze of pain and misery.

"We should arrive by dawn if we don't run into any trouble. Not that I think we will." The gate rattles as he opens it wider. "My kin all too busy fucking and drinking to pay you any attention."

I tie my hair into a ponytail, shrug the empty backpack onto my shoulder, and then I glance around the dungeon. To think I'll soon be free of this prison forever. Not even the threat of death would bring me back here.

A nervous flutter upturns my stomach. "What about Killian?"

Fenrik steps aside and nods for me to come out. "Don't worry about him. You won't be seeing the Dark Alpha any time soon."

For some inexplicable reason, a pang of guilt threatens to creep over me.

"What did you do to him?" I ask, swallowing the uneasy feeling rising from the depths of my stomach.

Fenrik regards my reaction through shrewd eyes. "Nothing I would've liked. He's just busy getting fucking some twins is all. Now, unless you wanna fill that role for the rest of your life, Zoriah, let's get the fuck out of here."

I push away any feelings of guilt, anger, or jealousy, and follow him outside.

Instead of leading me the usual way, he takes a sharp right at the exit and guides me through an archway leading on to another door at the far end. It's carved into the wall as if to hide it, but when Fenrik places his palm against the black stone, bright, glowing magical symbols appear. While I don't recognize their meaning, I'm smart enough to know it's an incantation, but it doesn't make sense.

"I thought only mages could do magic?" I say, genuinely mesmerized.

He winks over his shoulder. "There's a lot of things you don't know about me." Then he pulls his hand back and the entrance opens up into a dim passageway. "But there's also a lot I don't know about you... yet."

I follow him down the passageway. We must be under another building going by the footsteps banging on the ceiling. "There's not much to know, really. My parents died when I was young, and apparently it wasn't at the hands of your alpha, but at the hands of my former one. You know, the psychopath who tried sacrificing me? Yeah, him. I'm also deathly allergic to cats."

He huffs at the last bit. "A wolf who's allergic to cats? All right. Now I've seen it all."

"Trust me. You haven't seen anything yet."

Now his huff turns into genuine laughter. "I'll have to keep a close eye on you when we're mated, then." He slides a glance over his shoulder, winking at me. "Don't want the mother of my pups injuring herself."

My heart does a little dance against my ribs. Well, of course he'd want to breed with me. I'm to become his mate, and if he's to lead a successful pack, he'll need heirs. Many of them. Funny how I never thought about having pups until now. Not even Solas had mentioned breeding. Now that I think about it, that was a major red flag, but I failed to pick up on it.

Or perhaps I did and I was just in denial.

Wanting to honor your dead parents by mating with their alpha can do that to you.

I mean, becoming Solas' mate was all I've thought about since I was thirteen because I honestly believed it was the only way to make my parents proud. I cringe at how naive and blind I've been these past eight years. And I've been an alpha all along. My parents would be proud of that alone. At least, I hope so.

I hope they understand why I've done the things I have and why I'm here: it's to save Tristan and avenge every one of them, including myself. I fix my gaze on the end of the passageway. We emerge through another exit that leads up a stone staircase and into the shadows of the forest. It must've been an emergency escape route of some kind.

I pause and close my eyes then take a deep breath of the twilight air.

Freedom has never smelled so wonderful.

"Ready?"

Opening my eyes, I give him an affirmed nod.

"Then shift and follow me. There's a lake about ten miles east. We'll need to pass through it to reach the border. I hope you don't mind being cold."

I groan and prepare myself. "Let me guess. This lake is one of the magical ones your goddess blessed in all her divinity, which ironically makes us freeze to death when we swim through it?"

His mouth twitches. "The very one." Shrugging his pack back to the ground, he takes a step back. "Shift and try not to drown."

"Yeah, sure," I all but grumble at him. "I just hope we don't bump into any nixies."

As beautiful as the water sprites are, they're devious little creatures who won't think twice about trying to drown you. It's why we tend to avoid their land as much as possible. Not only that, but their magic infused in the water makes you feel colder than a penguin's ass.

"Once we cross the river, we can shift back. The distance will have given us a good enough head start."

With that, Fenrik effortlessly shifts into the most beautiful wolf I've ever laid eyes on. My breath hitches at the sight of them. His black fur shimmers in the moonlight, which is normal for dark wolves, but there's streaks of gold running through his coat.

That is definitely not normal for any wolf.

Who, or rather what, is he?

Before I can voice my questions, he bites down on the backpack and takes off into the trees. I hurriedly shift and run after him, making a mental note to ask him later.

Some hours later, the lake emerges within sight. I keep my head above the surface and kick my paws through the water to the other side. Fortunately, nothing tugs on me while I swim. The nixies must be asleep or preoccupied with something else. Thank the goddess.

By the time we shift back and reach a spot Fenrik deems suitable enough to rest, my clothes are still wet and I can't stop shivering.

Fenrik places his backpack by the fire and glances at me rubbing my arms in an effort to thwart the chill.

"Come put your clothes by the fire," he says, jutting his chin toward the flames. There's a softness in his voice I've never heard until now. He reaches for his damp shirt and pulls it over his body, revealing a torso sculpted in muscles.

And scars.

Some of them look recent, too, with light bruising surrounding them. He must've gotten them from when the light wolves attacked. While Killian's chest is like a work of art, Fenrik's a canvas of pain and suffering. My breath hitches at the sight of all his battle wounds.

He catches me studying them and shrugs. "They received worse, trust me."

"I bet they did," I murmur, looking away.

His softened voice cuts through the silence. "Answer me this honestly, Medley. Do you trust me?"

I glance back at him curiously. Do I trust the wolf who freed me from a cage and promised to set Tristan free, too?

"I'm not entirely sure," I answer quietly. "But I want to."

He lays his shirt on the rock by the fire and nods. "Then we're off to a good start."

I stand and reach for the hem of my dress, hesitating only briefly. "A much better one than the one I had with Killian, that's for sure."

He laughs at that and scratches his stubble. "I never did understand how you crept up on us that day. Never saw Killian lost for words before, either. How'd you do it?"

His intense gaze is fixed on me. It's silly to want him to turn around while I undress. It's not like I can hide my body after I remove my clothes, but I do need them to dry. It should help a little with trying to lose our scent.

When I glance around the clearing, Fenrik bends near the fire to add more kindling, his attention diverted from me. I smile at the small gesture of privacy and remove my dress.

"Focus, commitment, and sheer fucking will," I reply.

A smile this time, slightly lopsided. "Those skills will come in handy when we break your friend out," Fenrik replies. He removes his pants and sets them beside the shirt, followed by his socks, leaving him naked apart from his boxers. "We'll get a couple of hours rest and then hit the road again. We should reach the border by dawn."

I nod and place my clothes by the fire. The flames dancing over his face cast him in a warm glow that softens his rough edges a little. I almost can't believe this is the wolf I've promised to spend the rest of my life with. The moment we're officially mated under a full moon, he'll be as much mine as I'm his. Is that what I truly want though?

Killian's face seeps into my mind. If I had the choice, I'd choose no one, especially none of these wolves. The thought of mating and binding myself to someone now fills me with unease. The last time I did want to mate, he betrayed me in the most horrific way possible.

How can I be sure Fenrik won't do the same?

Or even Killian for that matter?

I guess I can't be sure which is why this is so terrifying to me.

A tendril of unease creeps through my body, but I remind myself that I'm an alpha. Whatever happens to me, I'll divide and conquer as I've always done.

"Still cold?"

Fenrik's voice brings me back to reality, and I blink at him. "A little."

"Lie in front of me by the fire. I'll keep your back warm."

I chuckle, but there's a nervous note in it. "Is keeping my back warm code for let's get our freak on?"

His gold eyes dilate, and an almost dark look flits over his expression. "As much as I want to claim you right now, I'm a wolf of my word. We will only mate once I have fulfilled my end of the bargain and not a second before."

I take a sharp inhale, nod, and walk over to him. He

continues stoking the fire while I lie on the moss-covered ground, my body angled slightly toward him. He straightens and moves over to check our clothes. Satisfied they're beginning to dry out, he grabs his gun from his backpack and walks over to me.

For some silly reason, I hold my breath and wait for him to lie down. It takes him several moments, and I don't know what he's doing. Hopefully checking we're still alone.

After a minute of silence and still no movement, I ask, "Are you not going to sleep?"

"No," he replies, settling down beside me. "I'll keep watch."

My lips tilt in a smile. Fenrik always seems to be keeping watch over me, but this time it's of his own accord and of mine too.

11

ZORIAH

I close my eyes by the fire and try to relax my muscles. When Fenrik stretches out behind me, I half expect him to go back on his word and take me into his arms. But he doesn't. He refrains entirely from placing so much as a finger on my body, which is surprising. There was a part of me that doubted his restraint; his alpha hardly set a good example of that.

However, the heat from Fenrik's body warms my back while the crackling fire warms my front. Slowly the urge to sleep takes over me, but when I close my eyes, all I see is Killian's face smirking at me. Even the memory of his lips on mine, his hands exploring my body, his cock pulsing inside me, filter through my mind. I turn on my back and clench my lids tighter.

Stop thinking about him, stop thinking about him.

Killian is an asshole.

The very definition of an alphahole.

For what feels like an eternity, I toss and turn while repeating this in my mind. Nothing works. My eyes grow heavy from exhaustion and my body, despite Fenrik's closeness, starts to shiver. I let out a frustrated huff of air and scuttle closer to the fire. But no matter what I do, I can't seem to get any more heat into my body which is one of the reasons I can't fall asleep. It's like Killian's taunting me even though I'm no longer his captive anymore.

"Trouble sleeping?"

Fenrik's deep voice washes over me. He's so close that his breath fans the back of my neck, tickling me.

I turn my head toward him. "What gave you that impression?"

He arches a slightly scarred brow. "Dunno. Maybe all the huffing, puffing, tossing, and turning, muttering under your breath. Or perhaps it was the—"

"Okay, I get it. Yes, I'm having trouble falling asleep."

"Well, try harder. You need your strength if we're to rescue your friend when it's just the two of us."

I bite my lip and stare at the stars. He's right. "Then what do you suggest?"

He gives a half-shrug. "Beating the meat always helps me."

I huff at that. "Yeah, I bet it did. Are you suggesting getting our freak on will help me fall asleep?"

When I peek at him, his eyes are already on me, the pupils blown with something dark and lustful.

Slowly, he wets his lips. "I don't mind lending you a hand, Medley, or a tongue. Just saying."

I close my eyes with a sigh, though his reply does make me laugh through my nose. "How very fucking noble of you."

He chuckles, and damn, it's sexy.

I wished he'd done it back at the dark wolves' main base. It would've made my captivity just that tiny bit more tolerable. Although, he never did hide the fact that he finds me appealing to look at. Especially the time he watched me bathe.

I turn on my side and rest my head on my arm. "You're a bit shameless, aren't you?"

He turns, too, but he rests his head in his palm while his elbow rests on the ground. "You gotta be in our realm. Plus, I'm not the kind of wolf to beat around the bush, unless I've got my tongue inside it."

A blush warms my cheeks. And then, before I fully register what I'm doing, I swat him playfully on the arm as though he were a good friend.

As though he were Tristan.

Fenrik's cheeks dimple as his lips spread into a full-blown smile; the kind that reaches his eyes. I think this is also the first time I've ever seen him smile, and it suits him.

"You look different when you're not covered in blood," I murmur.

His smile falters slightly. "You think I want to look like that?" He scoffs and shakes his head. "That's just what the Shadowlands does to you. Turns you into a bloodthirsty monster."

"Is that why you want out?" I ask. "To start fresh?"

He tilts his focus skyward. "Not sure wolves like me can start fresh, but... I want to be in a position where I can give those who can one."

I stare at him, marveling how for such a ruthless wolf, he's not completely dark at his core. He catches me studying him and instead of looking away, he studies me too. His eyes trail every inch of my face and his pupils dilate when they land on my mouth. There's an intense yearning in his gaze that transmits from his body to mine, and an unexpected warmth spreads through me.

I swipe my tongue over my lips to wet them and

shimmy toward him. He plucks a twig from my hair and then reaches for my cheek. His touch is surprisingly gentle when he caresses me, but his voice is dark, almost dangerous. Exciting.

"If you lick your lips one more time, Zoriah, I'm going to find it fucking impossible not to go back on my word and touch you."

Perhaps a demon has taken possession of my body, because for whatever reason, I deliberately wet my lips in a slow motion.

Fenrik drags me into his arms, my back pressed close to his muscular chest, and his erection nudges me.

"You'll be warmer here," he says, sliding his hand up and down my arm, "and I always knew you were more vixen than wolf. Tempting me like that, you little minx."

I chuckle at him. "I'm just cold and tired, is all."

"Uh-huh. Well, your pussy better be nice and wet, too, for what I'm about to do to you."

Oh, my sweet fuck. Did Fenrik just...? Yep. Yep, he did say those things, and they were so freaking hot. I had no idea he could talk this much, especially so dirty to me, but then again, it suits him. Everything about Fenrik is ruthless, primal male, including his wicked tongue.

He brushes his lips against my ear and lightly grazes me with his teeth. "I want your pussy dripping, Zoriah. I won't claim you unless I know you're ready to be satisfied, so get wet. Or I'll use my tongue to devour every inch of your beautiful body."

I instantly squeeze my thighs and bite my lower lip, tempted to challenge his resolve. The wolf follows the movement with his eyes and a low, deep growl rumbles in the depths of his throat. My insides are already tingling just from his words. I have no doubt in my mind that if he were to reach between my legs this second, he'd find I've done exactly as he asked.

I'm already wet, waiting for him.

He slides his big hand down the curves of my body and over my stomach. His breath taunts my ear as he slides between my legs. With almost painful slowness, he glides his fingers over me and pries my lips apart, feeling for my wetness.

"It appears you can follow orders." He chuckles, and his warm breath tickles my neck. "Good girl."

I bite my lip and close my eyes. Focusing on the pad of his thumb massaging my clit, I surrender and give myself over to sensation. Fenrik's hardened cock presses against me, straining with need. I'm no longer surrendering to sensation anymore but once again to insanity, because right now, I want Fenrik to touch me.

And he does.

He snakes his other arm around me and cups my breast with a large, callused hand. The whisper of air breathing over the sensitive spot on my nape causes me to shudder and squirm against him. He caresses my nipple and teases my clit while adorning my neck in kisses. A warm, tingling sensation gathers in response to them and it swells into a crescendo that bursts from my lips in a series of moans. Fenrik's low chuckle fills the gaps of my breathing as I come down from my high.

"Now you will go to sleep," he murmurs, nibbling the side of my ear.

I smile sleepily at him and this time don't suppress my yawn. "Very well... alpha."

He freezes as though the word struck him. Oops. Maybe I touched a nerve? I thought he'd like me calling him alpha since that's what he wants to become.

"Fenrik, I didn't mean to—"

He grabs my jaw and kisses me, deep and passionately.

The air leaves my lungs as his powerful tongue takes purchase of my mouth. There's an urgency about his movements that I can't quite explain, but I don't really want to.

He's the first male I've ever kissed who I actually want to kiss me.

The chaste kiss Solas stole one night under the moon had been swift and unexpected. Killian's had practically been forced, ripped from the depths of my being. But Fenrik... he kisses me softly yet firmly, passionately yet fiercely. He's also the first who hasn't forced me to do, well, anything I don't want to do.

Fenrik offered, and I took, and now I'm completely at his mercy.

Ribbons of pale moonlight stretch through the trees and bleed over us, causing Fenrik's hair to look silver instead of blond. But his bronze skin...

"You're glowing," I say, touching the warm light radiating under the surface of his skin.

Fenrik doesn't appear fazed at all. "It happens sometimes."

"What causes it?"

He looks away, clearly wanting me to drop the subject. "Another time. We'll leave in a couple of hours and should reach the border at dawn. Get some sleep. Good night."

Before I can press him for more answers, he lies on his back to stare up at the moon and rests his arms behind his head. Despite that I want to know the reason behind his mysterious glowing, if perhaps he's part mage as well as light wolf, exhaustion tugs at me, and I let out a yawn.

"All right," I say, lying beside him, "but if we're going to

become mates, you'll have to be honest with me. No secrets.
Ever."

"No secrets," he repeats, catching my eye. "Ever."

Weirdly, I actually believe him and that scares me a
little.

I never thought I'd trust a dark wolf ever again.

THE MORNING LIGHT STREAMING OVER ME IS A PLEASANT WELCOME
in comparison to last night's coldness. But then a shadow
eclipses the sun and the warmth vanishes. I open an eyelid
to see what's blocking the sun only to regret waking up at
all when I find Killian growling down at me. I stare up into
his wolf's eyes, struggling to find the right words to say.

"Good morning. Fancy seeing you here," I mutter
lamely.

Probably not the best thing I could've gone with.

Killian snarls and brings his wrinkled nose within
inches of my face. Okay. So running away from Killian and
then getting found by said alpha is not how I planned to
start my day.

I side-glance Fenrik and my pulse accelerates even
faster when he's nowhere to be seen.

*Did he abandon me while I slept? Or did Killian do some-
thing to him?*

I whip my gaze back to the alpha and search him for
any blood, but his obsidian fur remains dry and bloodless.
Hopefully that's a good sign.

"Get... away from her."

Fenrik's calm, authoritative voice snaps the alpha's

head toward him. Opposite the dying fire, Fenrik stands facing us, dressed in only his pants. Droplets of water trickle down his bronze muscular chest, catching the dawn light. He throws an empty bottle of water aside and takes a step.

"I said get back, Killian. You will not win this fight."

The shift in Fenrik's tone, from beta to alpha, is as evident and powerful as the sun is in the clear-blue sky. He holds himself tall and looks Killian dead in the eye. His brother snarls at him and steps over me.

At that moment, Fenrik shifts and lunges for his brother.

Killian's slightly larger wolf goes for his neck while Fenrik digs his claws into the alpha's face and bites down on his side. Killian twists his body in an effort to slam Fenrik against the ground, but it doesn't keep him down for long. Killian goes for the underbelly and blood permeates the air, followed by a pain-filled yelp. I flinch in tandem with the sound. I can't just sit by and watch. They're fighting because of me, and as much as they both infuriate me—one more than the other—I don't want to be the cause of their deaths.

I get to my feet and prepare to shift, but then I realize I'm more vulnerable in my current form. If Killian wanted to injure me, I'm pretty sure he would've done so when he found me asleep, which means he doesn't want to hurt me. Putting myself at risk may be the only way to stop them. I'm not even wearing any clothes which makes me even more vulnerable. As they both circle each other slowly, I drag what I can of my clothes over my body and run forward, placing myself directly between them.

"*Stop!*"

12

KILLIAN

The last thread of my patience breaks when Zoriah steps in the way of my target.

She extends her arms in supplication but maintains a half-tilted posture to protect my brother. Of course she doesn't want me to hurt him. Their scents cling to each other, urging me to release my wolf on them.

If I were an alpha with a lesser amount of self-control, I would defend my territory by doing just that. I'd rip my brother into pieces for what he's done.

"Killian... Don't do this." She lowers her voice into a whisper. "There doesn't need to be a fight."

Tell that to the bastard behind you who betrayed me!

I shift back, my injuries instantly beginning to heal. "Step aside, female."

She holds her position in a futile act of dominance. However, the pungent smell of her fear gives her away. At least she's smart enough to be frightened of me. I wanted to kill her, too, when I found out what she did.

"We made a deal, Killian."

I bare my teeth in warning, my focus still on my brother. "That deal means nothing now that you have violated your part of the terms... with a traitor."

Fenrik snarls and prepares to lunge. Zoriah holds him back by placing a hand on his shoulder, causing a growl to rumble in my chest.

"I knew we had our differences," I spit at him, "but I never had you down as a coward. What's wrong? Too weak to fight me like a man?"

He lunges and sheds his wolf in the air.

Blood covers his body when he lands on the ground beside Zoriah, his clothes badly shredded by my claws. I knew calling him a coward would provoke him. It always does. He tightens his jaw, clenches and unclenches his right hand. The one that's always been weaker since I nearly cut it off the night he failed to protect my mother. If he hadn't abandoned his post, Solas never would have captured my mother...and she wouldn't have been mutilated beyond recognition. She'd probably still be alive too.

He steps in front of Zoriah and wraps an arm around her. "Enough with the games, Killian... How the fuck did you find us?"

I stare at the placement of his hand and grind my teeth. "I have my ways. You know more than anyone about the things I'm capable of." I lift my hand and dark, smoky tendrils bleed from my palm. "How about a little demonstration for old time's sake?"

The magic barely seeps into the air when he tries to shove the female back to protect her. I wrap the tendril around his throat and shove him aside. Zoriah runs to intervene, but I bind her wrists with more tendrils and hold her back. With my other hand, I slam Fenrik against the rocks and pin him there so he's forced to watch what's about to happen yet be powerless to do anything.

"This is what happens when you betray me." I reel Zoriah in and trap her with my arms. She scowls up at me but I only sneer down into her face. "You fucked up big, sweetheart, and now it's time to face the music."

She casts a furtive glance at Fenrik who's trying to shatter his bonds, but we both know it's impossible. Only the Dark Alpha can wield the Chains of Darkness after pledging their soul to the Moon God. It was Rvyiel who created the chains as a weapon to keep other alphas in line. One day I will use them on Solas.

For now my brother can try them on for size.

"Zo... ri...ah..." He yanks at the chains again while choking out her name. "Run."

I pin her with my stare. "Don't you fucking move. You've been spared so far only because I hunted you alone. Had I done otherwise, you'd be dead by now. Both of you."

She stares back at me, her eyes filled with an emotion I've never seen there before. Regret. "Then why haven't you killed us? What are you going to do?"

I pause to consider my reply because I'm not entirely sure why I'm dragging this out. I guess there's a twisted part of me that's enjoying all this after the night of hell they put me through. But if I'm being honest, I haven't decided what to do yet. Pack law demands I punish them in front of the pack. If I don't, and I let their crime go without severe punishment, my pack will start questioning my authority as alpha.

Fenrik will need to be exiled. He can live in the Lycan Woods and be eaten by the light wolves for all I care. The female, however... She will have to be dealt with the old fashioned way. This will all come later. More pressing is the matter of her current predicament. There's too many other shifters roaming this part of the realm that every second puts her in danger. The fact my brother camped here, out in the open, just pisses me off even more.

To risk his life is one thing.

To risk my future mate's is another altogether.

I need to get her somewhere safe.

I train my eyes back down on her. "Don't worry, female. I've got something extra special planned for you once we get home. As for your new lover?" I slide Fenrik a bitter look. "He knows exactly what happens to dark wolves who betray their alpha. Don't you... Brother?"

Despite everything, it's the last word that seems to catch in the female's mind.

She cranes her neck to look at him. "Brother?"

So he didn't tell her who he really was? Oh, gods, this is good. Too fucking good.

He pulls harder at his chains, his attempts growing more frantic but stronger.

It only makes me chuckle. "Oh, this is good. Too fucking good, Brother. You didn't tell her?" I step back from the female, keeping her tethered to me like a leashed pup, and shift over to my brother's side. "Allow me to introduce you." I seize his foot and pull down, causing the bonds around his neck to strain and tighten. "Believe it or not, this son of a bitch right here is my older brother. He's also the true Dark Alpha of the Shadowlands." Curling my lips backward in a disgusted sneer, I dig my claws into his flesh. "Or rather, he would've been, if his mother wasn't a light wolf whore who betrayed our father. Isn't that right, Fen?"

He twists his neck, straining the veins pulsing in his throat, and bellows a deafening roar. A flicker of amber light gathers in the center of his chest then. It builds slowly and burns a path up his throat. When it explodes from his mouth, it releases a shockwave so powerful it knocks me off balance. Zoriah screams as she, too, is dragged off her feet.

She lands in a coughing heap beside me, her shocked expression mirroring the surprise I feel inside. This has never happened to Fenrik before. It wouldn't—couldn't—because he's not an alpha. He did not bleed upon the altar and pledge eternal allegiance to Ryviel, who, in return, would give him with the power of darkness.

There is nothing dark or natural about Fenrik's power.

He must've come into it a different way.

Another shockwave shoots out from him.

I grip my fingers into the dirt for support and brace myself for the impact. Zoriah holds on to my arm which instantly causes my skin to flare at the contact—even now, with the threat of death looming over me. Does she have any idea what she does to me? Or how close I came to killing my own brother over her?

"Go home, Brother," Fenrik bellows, his entire body engulfed in flames. "Leave before I bathe this ground in your blood."

He's no longer pinned to the rock but walking toward me. Molten ribbons bleed from his eyes and wrap around his chains, one by one shattering them into nothing.

Zoriah makes a move to go to him.

"Stay back," I warn and grab her by the arm. "My brother may be possessed by a fire demon."

She tries to shrug me off. "He's not possessed. He's pissed."

"So am I, but I'm not glowing."

Fenrik snarls and the flames devouring him grow brighter and hotter. The momentary distraction costs me the grip on Zoriah, and she frees herself to once again stand between us. The only difference this time is that I never would have hurt her. But I can't say the same for my brother. The flames begin to pulse erratically, and his face contorts as he struggles to control them.

"Zoriah, get back!"

The heat radiating from my brother is damn near searing even from here. Yet she keeps walking to him with her arm outstretched.

"Fenrik won't hurt me. He's... he's my friend."

"Oh, he's just a friend, is he?" I snarl at her blatant hesitation.

Like fuck he is.

However, the desperation in her voice does something to Fenrik. He sways on his feet and his fire loses some of its intensity.

"Fenrik, listen to me," she calls out. "We don't have the time to fight. That can come later."

My little wolf has no idea how right she is. I have every intention of picking up where we left off as soon as I get her home.

And I do not intend to lose.

Not even if Fenrik summons his fires from the pits of Hell itself.

When the female is close to touching him, the flames dim further like the last embers dying over a grate.

"Fenrik, I don't want to do this either, but we need to stop fighting. We need to work together. My friend's life depends on it." She places a hand on his shoulder, and the fire seeps back into his skin until nothing remains.

"Gods save me from your *friends,* little mate," I grumble under my breath. "What the fuck does the imprisoned *friend* do? Shoot ice out his ass? If so, please, let's hurry because this I've gotta see before he gives up the ghost."

The female glares at me from over her shoulder. "Tristan is not dead, and I am *not* your mate. As it stands, I won't be anyone's mate if no one here is capable of honoring their deal."

The audacity of this female truly knows no bounds.

Then again, even if it did, she'd probably cross them on purpose just to piss me off.

"Why would I honor my part of the deal after you so thoroughly violated yours?" I ask.

"Because you were the one who violated the deal first," Fenrik replies.

Although he's not glowing anymore, the rage burning in his eyes for me is no less searing.

Zoriah looks me dead in the eye. "And I'm not going back with you until Tristian is free."

"You make it sound like you have a choice," I scoff at her. "What's to stop me from dragging you back by the scruff of your neck?"

Fenrik steps forward. "I am."

To my utter delight, Zoriah slaps his arm and skirts around him. "Will the two of you stop pushing me around? I'm done being treated like a doll. Either we go together, or I go without you. And before you say anything, Killian, at least I'm giving you a choice."

For a long while, no one speaks and the silence turns into a staring contest between us males. The female just rolls her eyes.

"Are you going to measure your dicks next or see who can piss the longest? Let me save you some time. While I can't confirm the winner of the former, if we don't start getting a move on soon, I can confirm that neither of you will be able to do the latter after I'm done with you."

I stare at my brother with a look of awe mixed with amusement. "I tell you what, brother. She's been spending too much time with you. You've damn near corrupted her."

Finally, a glimpse of the old Fenrik returns, a faint hint of a smirk. ` "Zoriah is right. We stand a better chance of infiltrating Solas' compound together."

"No," I growl. "Zoriah is not coming with us."

Predictably, my words send her into a fit of rage. She takes a deep breath and prepares to unleash hell on me.

"I am *not* risking your life, Zoriah."

She releases her breath and frowns at me. "What? Just so you can keep your advantage over the light wolves?"

I let the silence speak for me because the truth is, if something takes Zoriah from me, Fenrik's flames will pale in comparison to the inferno I'll unleash upon the Four Realms. Not even the gods themselves will be able stop me.

Zoriah is mine. My female. My mate.

But if she ever suspected the lengths I'd go to for her, she'd become impossible to deal with. Already she thinks she can order me around and make demands of me as if she's my alpha. The truth and depth of my desire for this stubborn female will just become another weapon in her arsenal.

"Either Fenrik and I leave now, without you, or you let your friend suffer even more. See? I'm also capable of giving you a choice."

My brother nods and turns to her. "There is a safe zone on the border. You will wait for us there."

"Go on. Argue again and lose more time that your friend does not have," I say.

But she doesn't.

Fenrik tilts her chin and the brazen display of their intimacy sets my blood to boil. He'll pay for that later.

"Trust me, Zoriah?"

She stares up at him, searching his face until something flickers in her expression. "Trust is earned. Saving my friend will bring the two of you a step closer."

13
ZORIAH

Fenrik's parting words to me are still ringing in my head when I step over the threshold of the tavern. *"Keep your head low. The owner might look like a light wolf, but trust me when I say she screams like a banshee if you don't listen to it. So if she offers you something to eat, you eat it, and if she speaks to you, you just nod your head and hope it wasn't a question."*

Killian followed this up with a not so subtle warning. *"But if the old bat does ask you a question, you lie. Now for the love of gods, Zoriah, stay inside the tavern."*

He always has such a lovely way with words.

However, for once I do as I'm told and cover most of my face with the hood of Killian's cloak. But the tavern is small and crowded, making it difficult to slip inside unnoticed. The tantalizing scent of warm food is enough to relax my guard a little. It's been too long since my last hot meal. And my next one is not guaranteed, hot or cold.

It would be foolish to waste this opportunity.

A seat at the bar frees and I hurry to claim it. The overpowering smell of tobacco and ale cloying the thick air wraps around me as I squeeze a path through the various kinds of creatures. A dragon shifter blows a stream of hot air into his bowl to warm up the stew inside.

Heating up your own food in a public place is never a good sign.

Although at this rate, I'd eat anything thrown in front of me that's not moving.

I pull out the wooden stool and climb onto the tattered leather surface, still warm from its previous occupant. An old woman appears at the opposite side of the bar. Her head barely reaches the counter and she has more white hair veiling her than I do. She cranes her neck to offer me a friendly smile, but it fades when she takes a deeper look at me. I fight the urge to pull my sleeve down and wipe my face in case there's something on it.

I'm exhausted, starving, sore from sleeping on the ground, and worried sick about Tristan. Oh, and also trying not to contemplate the probability of Killian having killed Fenrik already. Caring about my appearance is a commodity I can hardly afford right now.

Let her spend a couple weeks in a dungeon and see if she can keep her pristine condition.

"I've seen that look before," she says, her voice surprisingly loud for such a tiny woman.

Ah. This must be the owner.

"What look?" I ask, returning the smile she gave me earlier.

"Frozen to the bone, hungry, and so exhausted you damn near fell off your feet. What you need is some of my rabbit stew and a lovely soak in a nice hot bath."

A bowl of stew appears in front of me as if by magic.

"Go on now, dear. Eat up. Once you're done, I'll take you

to a room upstairs and you can have a little rest. How does that sound?"

Remembering Fenrik's advice from earlier, I nod. "Wonderful. Thank you, umm...?"

"Izadel, dear, but you can call me Izza if you'd like." She winks at me and fills a tankard and sets it beside me. "Something to help you relax."

I wrap my fingers around the metal to warm them from the cold. The sweet aroma of mead betrays the tankard's contents and I drink it quickly, the liquid burning a pleasant path down my throat. Thankfully, Killian left a pouch of coins in his pocket to cover food and board. I doubt he'd mind if I spent some of it on alcohol.

Goddess knows I need a good drink.

Keeping one eye on my surroundings, I lift the bowl and all but inhale the stew. With my hunger momentarily abated, however, there's little to distract from my other concerns. What if they're too late? What if Tristan is already dead?

No! I can't allow myself to think like that.

Izadel appears to notice my change in mood. It's like she's got a radar or something.

"Right, my lovely darling. I have the room ready and the bath waiting for you."

I slide off the stool but it takes me a moment to find my balance. "About the payment—"

Izadel places a soft, liver-spotted hand on my shoulder to steady me. Although if I were to fall, I'd probably take her down with me. "Don't you worry about that, dear. Let's just get you settled in."

She ushers me toward the staircase before I can insist any further. Maybe she's being genial because we're both light wolves. Whatever the reason, I'll be sure to repay her kindness one day. She climbs the stairs first, each step creaking under her weight. Strange. She looks like she weighs less than me. But I should know appearances can be deceiving.

Izadel leads the way down a narrow hallway with wooden doors on either side.

Pausing outside the second last door on the left, she produces a key from her pocket and slots it into the metal lock.

"Here we are now. You'll find everything inside including some towels and soaps." She leans on the key to get it to turn, then opens the door with a grunt. "If you need anything else, just let me know."

I nod dazedly as the warmth of the room beckons me in. The fire at the hearth sends my thoughts westward with Fenrik. It's difficult to accept that the wolf who freed me from my cage is also Killian's brother. But I can understand why he chose to hide this from me. I would've been more suspicious had I known his true identity and less likely to go with him.

The other thing he concealed from me, and everyone else, is still too mind-boggling to wrap my head around. The true extent of his power is a sight to behold, and frankly quite terrifying. Judging by his flicker of surprise when the flames burst from his skin, he hadn't been aware of it either. That does make his deceit easier to bear.

"You know what?" Izadel pops her head around the doorway. "I have some healing oils you might like. You looked awfully bedraggled when you first walked in. They'll help you sleep, too."

She doesn't wait for a response and simply hums her way back down the stairs.

With a smile, I close the door behind her and twist the

lock. I remove the cloak and place it at the foot of the double bed. In an adjoining room, I discover something that almost makes me weep. A wooden tub placed before another fire. It calls me to it and I immediately shed my clothes. Seconds later I climb in and sit back with a sigh.

The water is nearly scalding, but I'm not moving for all the gold in the Arithym.

Gods, I've needed this.

I drape my arms over the edge and rest my head against the tub, letting the water wash away the grime and dust of the road. The heat permeates my body and even without the oils she promised the experience is divine. This is the first time in weeks I've been left alone in a place I can feel at ease and safe. It's so good it almost has an illusion-like quality. One waiting for the right opportunity to burst and leave me cold and starving again.

The turning of the lock draws my attention.

Huh? I thought I'd locked it.

"It's just me with the oils, dear."

I straighten and pull my knees to my chest, trying to preserve some sense of modesty, which is ionic considering what I've been through and what I've done with Killian.

And his brother.

I should get an extensive map of their family tree before stripping for anybody else.

Izadel enters the bathroom with a tray. "I'll leave them by the tub. Also brought you this." She waves a half-burned candle. "I've found the scent to be quite intoxicating and relaxing for young wolves such as you."

Oblivious to my nakedness, the old woman sets the items on the floor beside me. A scented mist stems from the freshly lit candle, and I have to admit it does wonders for my frayed nerves. The calming fragrance nudges something awake in my mind.

Where have I smelled this before? It's like Munelites but different.

I search my memory but my vision blurs, distorting my train of thought, until I can't even scream for help. The water pulls me under and my lungs clamp in a desperate battle for air.

Strong hands break the surface and drag me out, dropping me in a coughing, spluttering mess on the floor. The last thing I hear before everything goes black is the Light Alpha's smug voice taunting me.

"There's been a change of plans, little lamb..."

Ready to find out what happens next?
Book 2 is now available!

BONUS SCENE

Ever wondered what happened when Zoriah tried to kill the Dark Alpha (the second time)? As a thank you for your support, you can read the exclusive bonus prequel for free here https://dl.bookfunnel.com/vv5vbxfxtx!

ABOUT THE AUTHOR

Scarlett Snow comes from a big family in a small Scottish town and has always strived to prove that if you are passionate about something, no one can stop you from chasing your dreams. She writes a variety of romance novels that range between Fantasy, Paranormal, Reverse Harem, Sci-fi, and M/M, and they usually have some delicious darkness thrown into the mix.

If you'd like to join her newsletter to be kept updated on her books, you can do so here: www.wintersnowpublishing.com

FOLLOW SCARLETT

Reader Group: https://www.facebook.com/groups/scarlettscoven
Facebook Page: https://www.facebook.com/authorscarlettsnow
Instagram: https://www.instagram.com/scarlettsnowauthor/
Amazon: https://www.amazon.com/Scarlett-Snow/e/B07NKFPSKN

OTHER BOOKS BY SCARLETT

Scarlett also writes under Kyra Snow (Male/Female Scifi Romance) and Katze Snow (Male/Male Dark Romance):

Katze: https://www.amazon.com/Katze-Snow/e/B01M0GTAED

Kyra: https://www.facebook.com/kyrasnowauthor

(Please not that Kyra no longer writes in the Elemental Mates universe and that all rights & exploitation of those rights have been assigned to her former co-writer. If you enjoy sci-fi and would like to support Kyra there, please check out her book RUTHLESS.)

Printed in Great Britain
by Amazon

75747118R00080